First published 2021 by North Parade Publishing Limited
3-6 Henrietta Mews
Bath
BA2 6LR, UK

Copyright © North Parade Publishing Limited, 2023

Predominant artwork and imagery source: Shutterstock.

All rights reserved. No part of this publication may be reprinted, stored in a retrieval system or transmitted in any form or by any means, electronic, mechanical, photocopying, recording, or otherwise, without the prior permission of the copyright holder.

500 Fantastic Facts
Space

Contents

1.	The Universe	08
2.	Origin of Universe	10
3.	Astronomy: Ancient	12
4.	Astronomy: Modern	14
5.	Geocentric and Heliocentric Models	16
6.	Ancient Astronomers	18
7.	Medieval and Renaissance Astronomers	20
8.	Modern Astronomers	22
9.	Telescope	24
10.	Hubble Space Telescope	26
11.	James Webb Telescope	28
12.	Galaxies	30
13.	Milky Way Galaxy	32
14.	Black Holes	34
15.	Nebulae	36
16.	Pulsars	38
17.	Star: Birth	40
18.	Star: Death	42
19.	Formation of Solar System	44
20.	Constituents of the Solar System	46
21.	The Sun 1	48
22.	The Sun 2	50
23.	Meteoroids	52
24.	Comets	54
25.	Asteroid	56
26.	Asteroid Belt	58
27.	Inner Planets: Terrestrial Planets	60
28.	Outer Planets: Gas Giants	62
29.	Outer Planets: Ice Giants	64
30.	Natural and Artificial Satellites	66

31.	Mercury 1	68
32.	Mercury 2	70
33.	Missions to Mercury	72
34.	Venus 1	74
35.	Venus 2	76
36.	Missions to Venus	78
37.	Earth 1	80
38.	Earth 2	82
39.	Moon 1	84
40.	Moon 2	86
41.	Moon Landing	88
42.	Mars 1	90
43.	Mars 2	92
44.	Mars's Moons	94
45.	Missions to Mars	96
46.	Jupiter 1	98
47.	Jupiter 2	100
48.	Jupiter's Moons	102
49.	Saturn 1	104
50.	Saturn 2	106
51.	Saturn's Moons	108
52.	Missions to Jupiter and Saturn	110
53.	Uranus	112
54.	Neptune	114
55.	Moons of Uranus and Neptune	116
56.	Missions to Uranus and Neptune	118
57.	Dwarf Planets	120
58.	International Space Station	122
59.	Famous Astronauts	124

The Universe

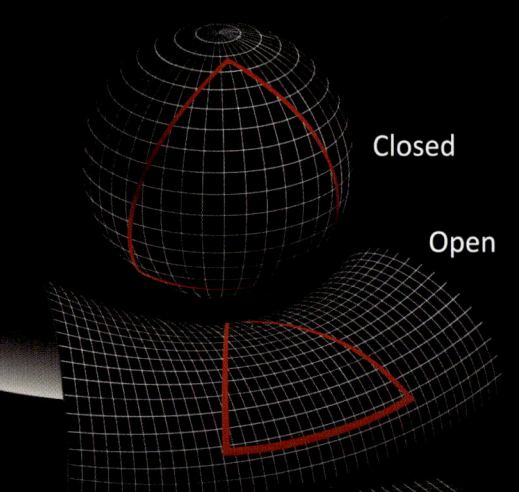
Closed
Open
Flat

01 The universe is the sum total of all existence. The universe includes all of space, matter, energy, and time. It has no centre or outer edge. The universe is infinite, and the size of the observable universe is currently about 93 billion light-years in diameter.

02 Depending on the density and expansion rate of the universe, its shape could be closed, open or flat. A dense universe would curve itself into a closed shape. The universe might take the open shape if it is not dense enough. The optimum amount of matter would give the universe a flat shape.

03 Although the universe is a limitless dark void, it is not empty. It contains trillions of stars, billions of galaxies, countless planets, moons, asteroids, comets, and clouds of dust and gas.

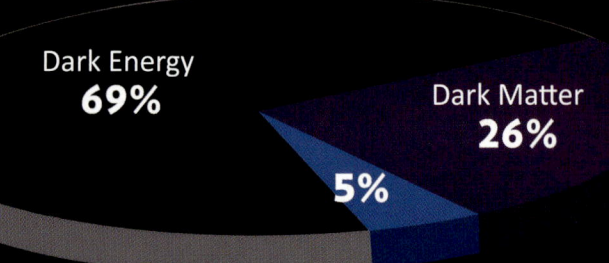
Dark Energy 69%
Dark Matter 26%
5%

04 Astronomers have found a huge water cloud in space about 12 billion light-years away from Earth. It is estimated that the water cloud contains 140 trillion times as much water as all the seas and oceans on Earth combined.

05 The two basic components of the entire universe are matter and energy. The observable matter makes up somewhere between 3 and 5 percent of the universe and is called normal matter. About 95 percent of the universe comprises dark matter and dark energy which are unobservable.

06 When we look into space, we are actually looking back in time. Light takes time to travel. The stars or galaxies we look at are millions of light-years away. This means that the light emitted by that object is a million years old, or to put it another way, we are looking back a million years.

07 Space is silent as sound waves need a medium to travel. Sound waves are mechanical waves which are in the form of vibrating waves. The absence of particles (medium) in space prevents the sound from travelling.

08 Black holes are a place in spacetime where gravity is so strong that even light cannot escape. The universe is full of black holes of all sizes ranging from stellar (10-24 times the mass of the Sun) to supermassive (1,000 million suns).

09 To measure distances in space the speed of light is used as a standard. One light-year is nearly 10 trillion kilometres. To try to understand the scale of space let us go through the steps in our cosmic address: Earth, solar system, Milky Way galaxy, cluster of galaxies, supercluster, universe.

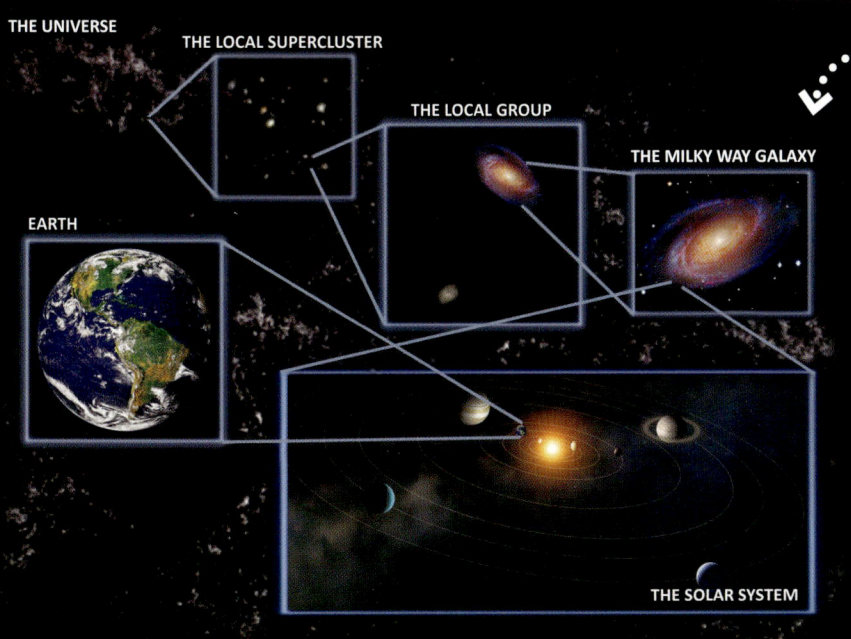

THE UNIVERSE
THE LOCAL SUPERCLUSTER
THE LOCAL GROUP
THE MILKY WAY GALAXY
EARTH
THE SOLAR SYSTEM

Origin of Universe

10 Before the origin of the universe all matter, space and energy were condensed into the size of a pinpoint called singularity. Around 13.8 billion years ago, the singularity suddenly expanded to a trillion kilometres across and the universe was born. This expansion of the space is called the Big Bang.

11 The Big Bang produced intense hot energy. In the initial moment of expansion, the universe was infinitely dense and incredibly hot. Within a tiny fraction of a second, the universe swelled from a size smaller than a subatomic particle to the size of a city.

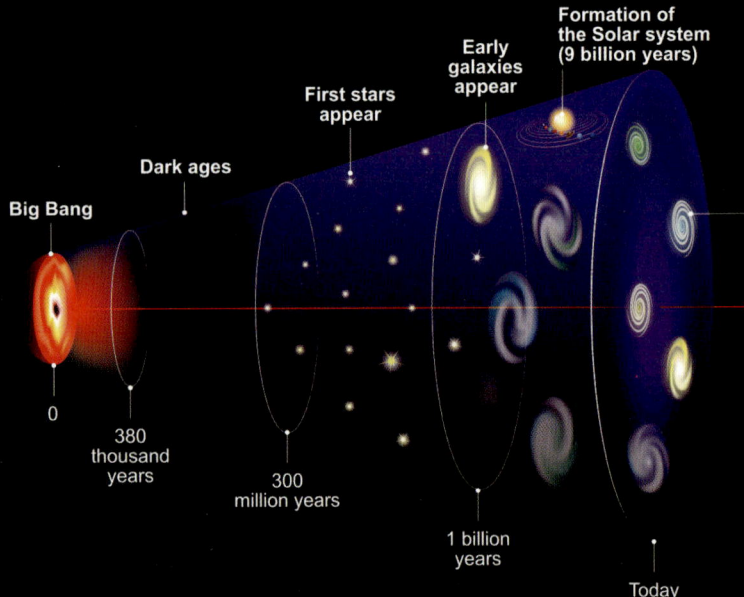

12 As the expansion continued, the universe slowly cooled and became less dense. About 300,000 years later, the universe cooled enough for atoms to form. The elements hydrogen and helium were created.

13 At 300 million years, gravity started acting on clouds of gases, pulling them into tight loops. Nuclear reactions were triggered by intense pressure and heat in the gaseous loops, resulting in the birth of stars. At 500 million years, the first galaxies started to form.

14 As space continued to expand, galaxy clusters and super clusters began forming. This period is called Structure Epoch, since it was during this time the modern universe began to take shape.

15 Georges Lemaître, a Belgian cosmologist and catholic priest, was the first person to propose that the universe was expanding. In a paper presented by him in 1927, he stated that the universe was initially a single particle which after an explosion stretched apart and is continuously stretching to this day. The theory was ignored by the scientists as Lemaître had no data to prove it.

16 In 1929, Edwin Hubble, an American astronomer, presented a paper based on his observational evidence for the expanding universe. Through a graph he showed that galaxies are moving back from us with a velocity that is proportional to their distance from us. This later came to be known as Hubble's law.

Steady-State Cosmology: Matter is constantly created as the Universe expands

 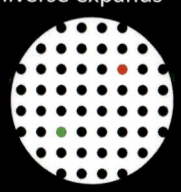 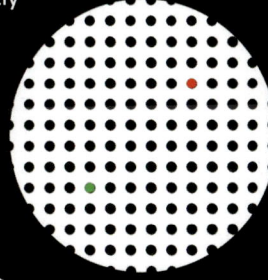

Big Bang Cosmology: Matter dilutes as the Universe expands

 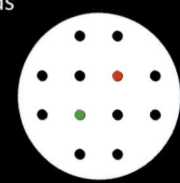 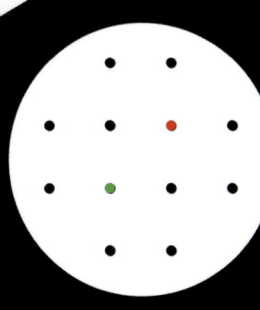

17 British scientists Sir Hermann Bondi, Thomas Gold, and Sir Fred Hoyle proposed the Steady-State theory in 1948, before the Big Bang theory was established. The theory states that the continuous creation of new matter keeps the density of matter in the expanding universe constant.

18 The discovery of "cosmic microwave background" in 1964, by Arno Penzias and Robert Wilson, proved to be the most important evidence for the Big Bang theory. This energy was the faded remains of the burst of energy released in the Big Bang.

Astronomy: Ancient

19 Astronomy, one of the oldest sciences, uses mathematics, physics, and chemistry to study the celestial objects such as stars, planets, comets, star clusters and galaxies and phenomena such as supernova, and cosmic microwave radiation.

20 A star chart is an astronomical map of the night sky. They served as a navigational aids in ancient times. The Dunhuang (China) star chart is the oldest and most accurate star map preserved in history.

21 Humans have always been fascinated and intrigued by the sky, Sun, Moon, and stars. Many ancient cultures worshipped the celestial bodies as gods. They followed them for navigation, catastrophic events and to keep track of the days and time of year.

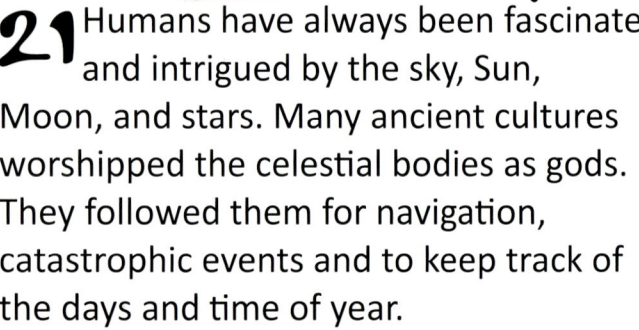

22 Ancient Egyptians were keen astronomers. The Great Pyramid of Giza was built to align with the North Star. The calendar developed by ancient Egyptians was a solar calendar. The year had 365 days divided into 12 months, with 30 days in each month.

23 The movement of celestial objects was meticulously tracked by the Mayans, who recorded it in astrological tables. They maintained precise charts that predicted eclipses, seasonal solstices, and equinoxes.

24 The Babylonians were the first to recognise periodicity in astronomical phenomena and maintained a daily record of the same. Even the sightings of the famous Halley's comet have been mentioned in their cuneiform tablets. The oldest surviving planetary astronomical text is the Venus tablet of Ammisaduqa in Babylonia.

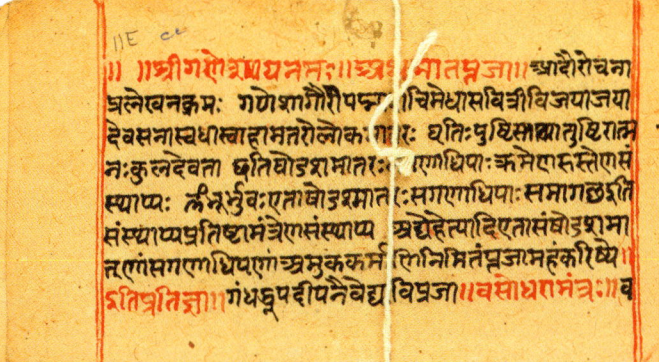

25 The earliest known Indian text on astronomy was *Vedanga Jyotisha* (1200 BCE). It details important aspects of time and seasons and describes rules for tracking the motion of the Sun and Moon. Aryabhata, Brahmagupta, Varahamihira and Bhaskara were some of the prominent ancient Indian astronomers.

26 Ever since people started stargazing, they have seen star patterns in the night sky. These star patterns, called constellations, have been given mythical and animal names by various cultures throughout human history. About 50 of the 88 constellations recognised by the International Astronomical Union (IAU) are attributed to the ancient Greeks.

27 In a quest to understand the working of the universe and the celestial bodies, Greeks extensively used mathematical equations, geometry, and geography. A mechanical device called "Antikythera Mechanism" was used by them to predict astronomical phenomena.

Astronomy: Modern

28 Observational astronomy gathers information through observations of celestial objects. Theoretical astronomy uses analytical models, based on physics and chemistry, for explaining astronomical phenomena. These two disciplines complement one another.

29 Radio telescopes are used in radio astronomy to pick up and amplify radio waves from space. These waves are then analysed to gain a better understanding of the universe.

30 An infrared spectrum is employed for examining objects that are too cold to emit visible light, such as planets, circumstellar discs, or nebulae. The Wide Field Infrared Survey Explorer (WISE) has helped in the observation of various numerous galactic protostars and their parent star clusters. The infrared observatories in space include the Spitzer Space Telescope, the Herschel Space Observatory, and the James Webb Space Telescope.

31 Astrometry is the oldest field in astronomy. It is the science that deals with the position and movement of celestial objects including planets, stars, asteroids, and galaxies. Careful measurement of the shift of position of a nearby star has helped us to measure the scale of the universe. Astrometry keeps track of near-Earth objects.

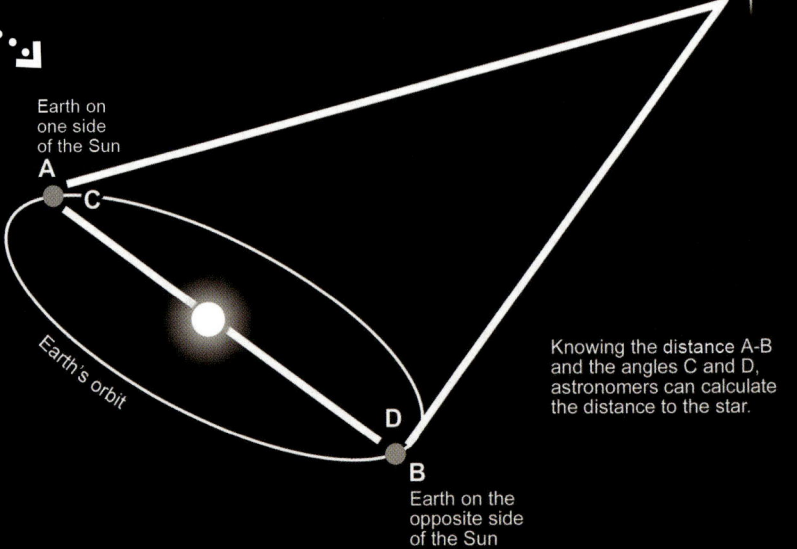

Star

Earth on one side of the Sun
A
C

Earth's orbit

D
B
Earth on the opposite side of the Sun

Knowing the distance A-B and the angles C and D, astronomers can calculate the distance to the star.

32 Astrophysics is the branch of astronomy that implements the principles of physics and chemistry to understand the birth, life, death, and nature of all the celestial bodies in our universe.

33 Astrochemistry is a combination of astronomy and chemistry. This discipline of science studies the atoms and molecules in space and their reaction with radiation. Astrochemistry helps us understand how the solar system and Earth was formed, the geology of Earth and how life originated.

34 Astrobiology is the study of life in the universe. This field of science is focussed on the study of origin, early evolution, distribution, and eventual fate of life in the universe. It also looks for extraterrestrial life and other worldly biospheres.

35 It was the invention of the telescope that revolutionised astronomy. The property of the telescope to collect light allows one to look farther than the naked eye can see. The two basic types of telescopes are: refracting and reflecting.

Geocentric and Heliocentric Models

36 The geocentric model of the universe places Earth at the center, with the Sun, Moon, stars, and other planets revolving around it. This model is often referred to as Ptolemy's geocentric model.

37 Eudoxus, the Greek mathematician and astronomer, was the first to suggest a geocentric model of the universe. His model was an intricate system of 27 interconnected, geo-concentric spheres, one for the fixed stars, four for each of the five planets, and three each for the Sun and Moon.

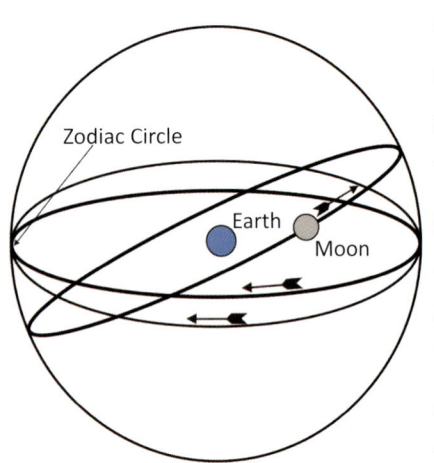

38 Aristotle, pupil of Plato and teacher of Alexander the Great, expanded on Eudoxus's model. His model had 56 instead of 27 spheres.

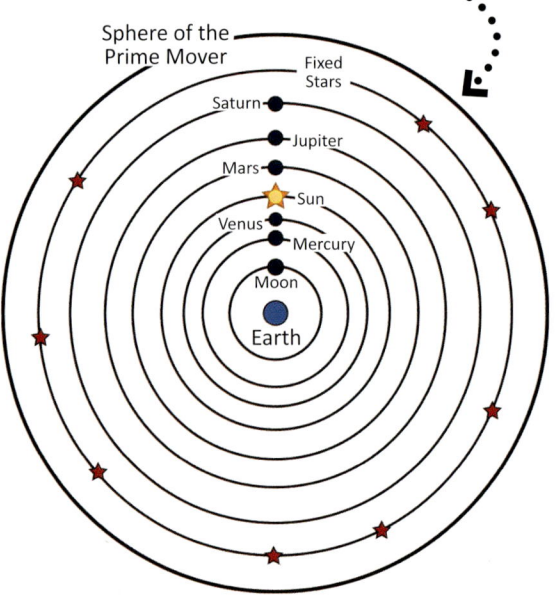

39 The most detailed but rather complicated geocentric model was provided by Egyptian-Greek astronomer Claudius Ptolemy. According to the Ptolemaic system, Earth was at the centre of the universe. Each of the other planets moved in a small circle known as an epicycle, the epicycle then moved around Earth in a larger circle known as deferent.

40 The Ptolemaic system explained the motion of planets and stars around Earth including the retrograde motion of planets. By using Ptolemy's tables, astronomers could accurately predict eclipses and the positions and locations of planets. Ptolemy's model remained the most widely accepted model for nearly 1,500 years because it matched the real visible events in the sky.

41 The heliocentric hypothesis (Helios means Sun) rejected the idea that Earth was at the centre of the universe; instead, it postulated that the Sun was at the centre, with all other planets, including Earth, orbiting around it.

42 Aristarchus of Samos, a Greek astronomer and mathematician, was the first to postulate that the Sun is the centre of the universe. His heliocentric hypothesis was based on the relative sizes of the Sun, Earth, and Moon as well as their distances from Earth.

43 Johannes Kepler and Galileo Galilei were the first few astronomers who supported the heliocentric model. Kepler, a German astronomer, made corrections in the Copernicus model by showing that the orbits of planets were elliptical rather than circular. Galileo's discovery of Jupiter's moons and Venus's phases further strengthened the heliocentric model.

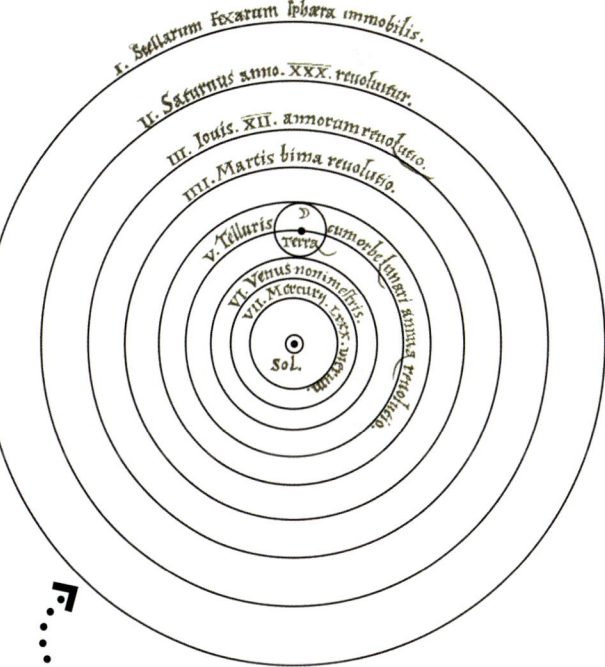

44 The heliocentric concept was first thoroughly developed by Polish astronomer Nicolaus Copernicus and the model was published in 1543. He also added that Earth rotates on its axis daily, revolves around the Sun once a year, and tilts its axis annually. The model's lack of accuracy in predicting planetary positioning prevented its widespread acceptance.

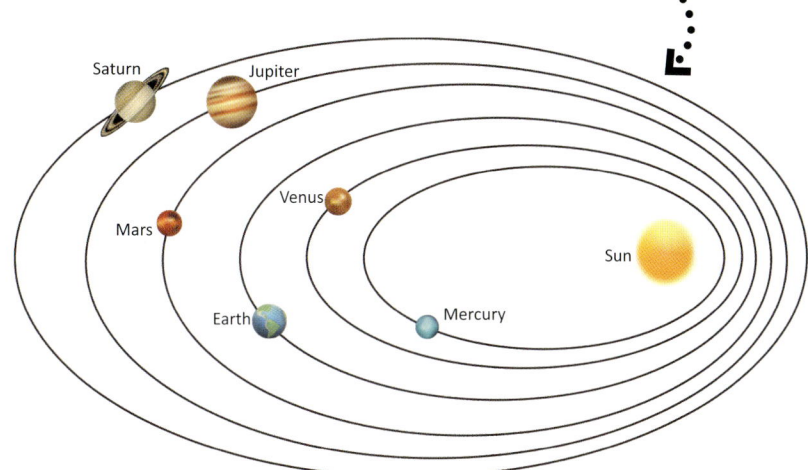

Ancient Astronomers

45 Democritus (460—370 BCE) was an ancient astronomer of Abdera. He believed that the world was composed of indivisible particles of matter (now known as atoms) and the whole cosmos was formed by these particles.

46 Aristotle (384—322 BCE), was one of the most influential Greek philosophers and scientists. He believed that Earth was a sphere in a spherical and finite universe and all the other celestial bodies revolved around it.

47 Aristarchus of Samos (310—230 BCE) was a Greek astronomer and mathematician. He was the first person to put forth a heliocentric model of the solar system. Some of Aristarchus's other achievements include correctly predicting Earth's rotation around its own axis and the invention of a sundial in the shape of a hemispherical bowl. His only surviving work is, *"On the Sizes and Distances (of the Sun and Moon)"*.

48 Eratosthenes of Cyrene (276—195 BCE) was a Greek polymath who excelled in astronomy, geography, and mathematics. He was the first person to calculate the circumference of Earth and its axial tilt. He used parallels and meridians to create a globe map in his book *Geographika*.

49 Hipparchus (190—120 BCE) was a Greek astronomer and mathematician. He created the first quantitative and precise models for the motions of the Sun and Moon. He had compiled the first star catalogue, and his use of numerical trigonometry enabled him to predict solar eclipses with great accuracy.

50 One of the finest minds of his time was the Egyptian-Greek astronomer, mathematician, and geographer Ptolemy (100–170 CE). His geocentric theory of the universe, also known as the Ptolemaic model, was accepted for 1,500 years, before it was proven false.

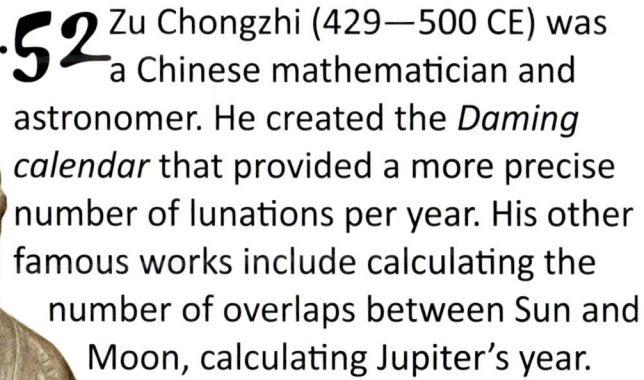

51 Hypatia of Alexandria (350/370—415 CE) was the first notable female astronomer and mathematician of her time. Her most significant works include the charting of celestial bodies, the invention of the astrolabe and an instrument to measure fluid (similar to a hydrometer).

52 Zu Chongzhi (429—500 CE) was a Chinese mathematician and astronomer. He created the *Daming calendar* that provided a more precise number of lunations per year. His other famous works include calculating the number of overlaps between Sun and Moon, calculating Jupiter's year.

53 Aryabhata (476—550 CE) was one of the great mathematicians and astronomers from the classical era in India. In his book, *Aryabhatiya*, he suggested that Earth was spherical and spins on its axis.

500 Fantastic Facts

Medieval and Renaissance Astronomers

54 Brahmagupta (598—670 CE) was the head of Ujjain's astronomical observatory, the prominent mathematical and astronomical centre of ancient India. His treatise, *Brahmasphutasiddhanta*, chiefly covers solar and lunar eclipses, planetary conjunctions, and positions of the planets.

55 Abd Al-Rahman Al Sufi (903—986 CE) was an outstanding Persian astronomer during the Middle Ages. He recorded the Andromeda galaxy in 964 CE and gave it the name "little cloud." This was the first instance of a star system discovered outside of our galaxy.

56 Muhammad ibn Musa al-Khwarizmi, better known simply as al-Khwarizmi (750—850 CE) was a Persian polymath. He is known as the father of algebra and his most notable work was the *Introduction of Hindu-Arabic Numerals*. The term *algorithm* comes from his name.

57 Bhaskaracharya (1114—1189 CE) also known as Bhaskar II, was an Indian mathematician and astronomer who continued the work of Brahmagupta at Ujjain's astronomical observatory. Regarded as the greatest mathematician of medieval India, he was also far ahead of his European contemporaries. He successfully calculated the length of the sidereal year.

58 Levi ben Gershon (1288—1304 CE) also known as Gersonides, was a French- Jewish philosopher and mathematician who invented an instrument, the Jacob's Staff, to measure the angular distance between celestial objects. He believed that the Milky Way was on the sphere of the fixed stars and shines by the reflected light of the Sun.

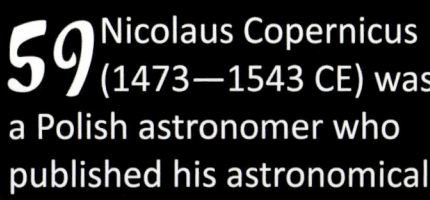

59 Nicolaus Copernicus (1473—1543 CE) was a Polish astronomer who published his astronomical model *Copernican heliocentrism* in 1543. According to this model, the Sun was at the centre of the universe while the five planets (known at that time) revolved around it.

60 Tycho Brahe (1546—1601 CE) was a Danish astronomer who practised observational astronomy. He designed and built numerous astronomical instruments and trained many young astronomers in the art of observing. He observed a supernova in 1572 and a comet in 1577 without the aid of a telescope.

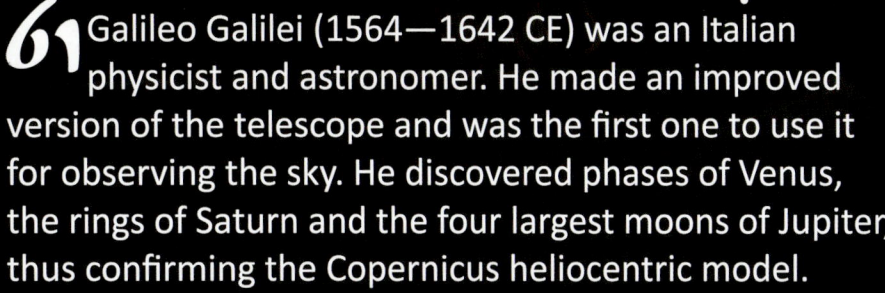

61 Galileo Galilei (1564—1642 CE) was an Italian physicist and astronomer. He made an improved version of the telescope and was the first one to use it for observing the sky. He discovered phases of Venus, the rings of Saturn and the four largest moons of Jupiter, thus confirming the Copernicus heliocentric model.

62 Johannes Keppler (1571—1630 CE) was a German mathematician and astronomer who made the discovery that Earth and the planets have elliptical orbits around the Sun. He gave three fundamental laws of planetary motion which are still in use. Though he assisted the famous astronomer Tycho Brahe, he was a follower of Copernican theory.

Modern Astronomers

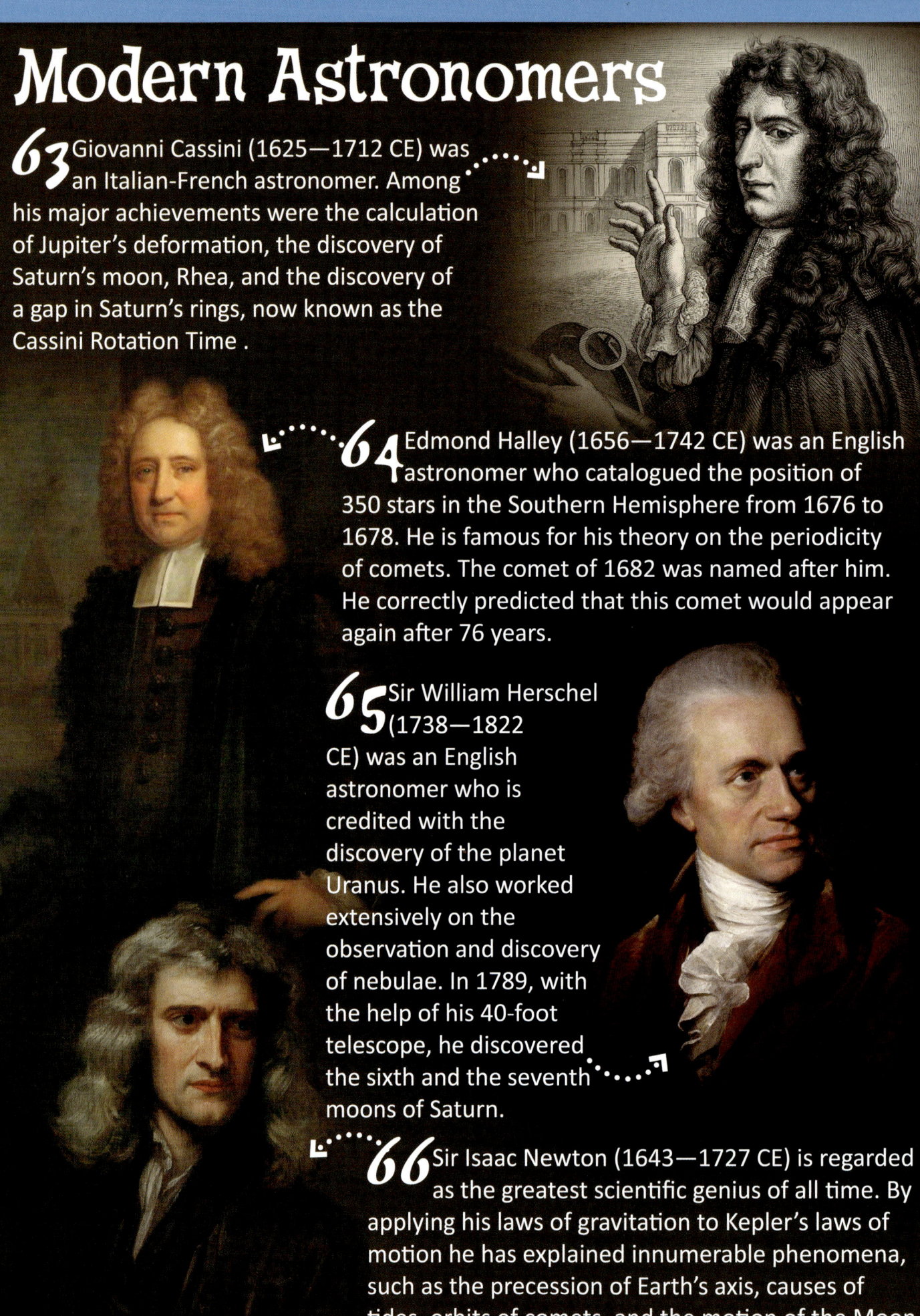

63 Giovanni Cassini (1625—1712 CE) was an Italian-French astronomer. Among his major achievements were the calculation of Jupiter's deformation, the discovery of Saturn's moon, Rhea, and the discovery of a gap in Saturn's rings, now known as the Cassini Rotation Time.

64 Edmond Halley (1656—1742 CE) was an English astronomer who catalogued the position of 350 stars in the Southern Hemisphere from 1676 to 1678. He is famous for his theory on the periodicity of comets. The comet of 1682 was named after him. He correctly predicted that this comet would appear again after 76 years.

65 Sir William Herschel (1738—1822 CE) was an English astronomer who is credited with the discovery of the planet Uranus. He also worked extensively on the observation and discovery of nebulae. In 1789, with the help of his 40-foot telescope, he discovered the sixth and the seventh moons of Saturn.

66 Sir Isaac Newton (1643—1727 CE) is regarded as the greatest scientific genius of all time. By applying his laws of gravitation to Kepler's laws of motion he has explained innumerable phenomena, such as the precession of Earth's axis, causes of tides, orbits of comets, and the motion of the Moon by the gravity of the Sun.

67 Albert Einstein (1879—1955 CE), a German-born theoretical physicist, was on par with Newton when it came to scientific achievements and discoveries. His theory of Special Relativity gave us the concept of spacetime. It has also helped scientists to understand the orbit of Mercury.

68 Srinivasa Ramanujan (1887—1920 CE) was a genius Indian mathematician who was exceptionally good in the field of infinite summation. Along with his mentor, G.H. Hardy, he did some exemplary work in mathematics. Ramanujan prime and Ramanujan theta function are now being used in finding out the complex properties of black holes.

69 Scottish astronomer Williamina Fleming (1857—1911 CE) is renowned for discovering the Horsehead Nebula and white dwarf stars. Using a classification system she created, she was able to catalogue thousands of stars.

70 Clyde Tombaugh (1906—1997 CE) was an American astronomer who discovered Pluto, the ninth planet (now dwarf) of our solar system on March 13, 1930. Over the next many years, he discovered two comets, six-star clusters, numerous asteroids as well as the vortex nature of Jupiter's Great Red Spot.

Telescope

Light focuses here — Large lens gathers and bends light

light

Small lens magnifies and focuses light for your eyes

71 Telescopes are optical devices that use lenses, mirrors, or a combination of both, to observe distant objects. The lens or the mirror collects light and uses it to form a magnified image of the object which is being seen.

72 The first record of a telescope comes from a patent filed in the Netherlands, in 1608, by a Dutch eyeglass maker, Hans Lippershey. The instrument could magnify things to three times their size. It had a concave eyepiece aligned with a convex objective lens.

73 Without ever having seen one, Galileo Galilei created one as soon as he learned about the "Dutch Perspective Glass." His device could magnify objects 20 times, making it superior to Lippershey's. With the help of this instrument Galileo discovered celestial features such as the Moon's craters, the rings of Saturn, and Jupiter's moons.

74 The two basic types of telescopes are: refracting and reflecting. The refracting telescope uses a convex lens whereas a curved mirror is used by a reflecting telescope. The earliest telescopes were mostly refracting.

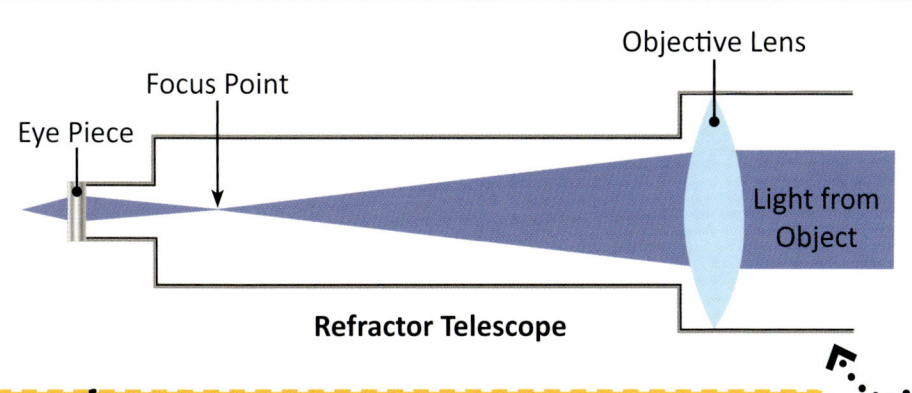

Refractor Telescope

75 In a refracting telescope, light entering the telescope is bent by the convex lens to focus it, creating an image. The image is then enlarged by the eyepiece, a small lens, at the opposite end of the telescope.

76 Giovanni Demisiani, the Greek theologist and mathematician, coined the word telescope for the instrument created by Galileo. The word "*teleskopos*" in Greek means "far-seeing".

77 In a reflecting telescope, light is reflected from a wide concave mirror onto a smaller flat mirror. The resulting image is then enlarged by an eyepiece lens.

Reflector Telescope

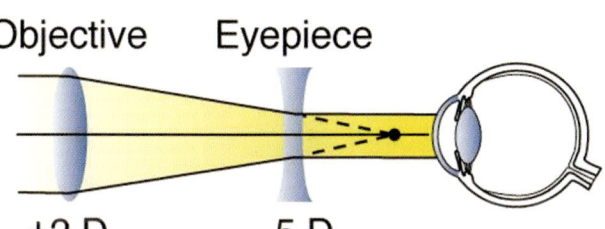

78 To better Galileo's design, Kepler used a convex lens for the eyepiece as opposed to Galileo's concave lens. Although this improved the view and the magnification, the images observed were inverted. It was accepted in the science community only by the middle of the 17th century.

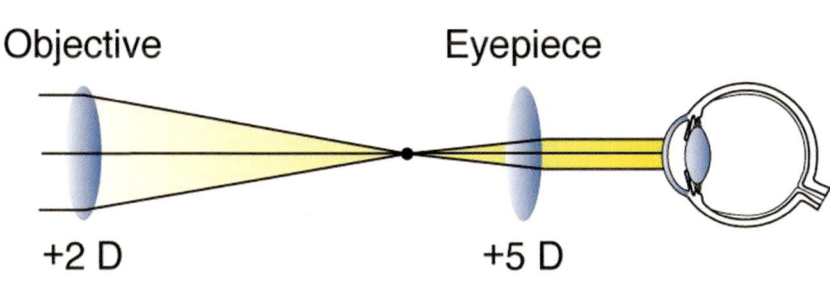

79 Sir Isaac Newton created the Newtonian telescope, the first functional reflecting telescope, in 1668. A concave primary mirror and a flat diagonal secondary mirror were used to design the telescope.

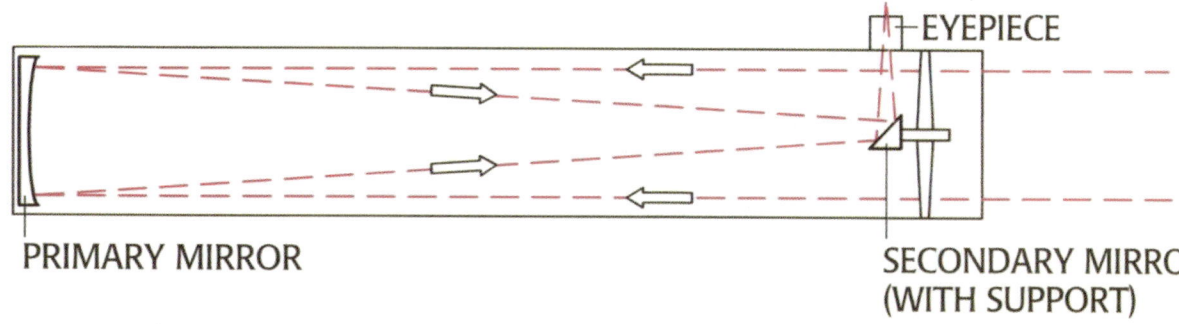

Hubble Space Telescope

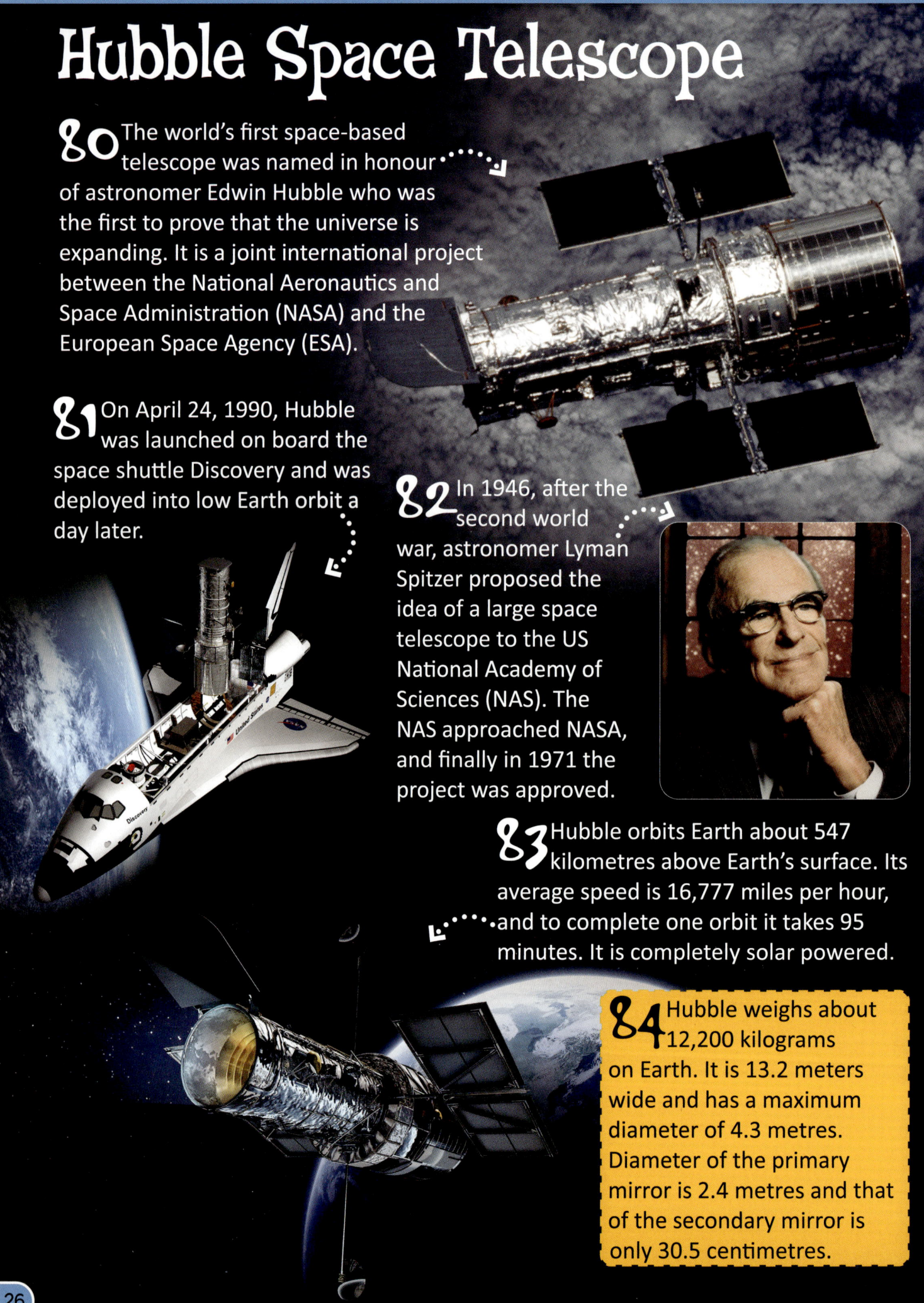

80 The world's first space-based telescope was named in honour of astronomer Edwin Hubble who was the first to prove that the universe is expanding. It is a joint international project between the National Aeronautics and Space Administration (NASA) and the European Space Agency (ESA).

81 On April 24, 1990, Hubble was launched on board the space shuttle Discovery and was deployed into low Earth orbit a day later.

82 In 1946, after the second world war, astronomer Lyman Spitzer proposed the idea of a large space telescope to the US National Academy of Sciences (NAS). The NAS approached NASA, and finally in 1971 the project was approved.

83 Hubble orbits Earth about 547 kilometres above Earth's surface. Its average speed is 16,777 miles per hour, and to complete one orbit it takes 95 minutes. It is completely solar powered.

84 Hubble weighs about 12,200 kilograms on Earth. It is 13.2 meters wide and has a maximum diameter of 4.3 metres. Diameter of the primary mirror is 2.4 metres and that of the secondary mirror is only 30.5 centimetres.

85 Hubble's latest discovery is "Earendel", which means "morning star" in old English. This star is around 28 billion light-years away from us and is the farthest star ever seen to date. In 2016, Hubble discovered GN-z11, the most distant galaxy, which is about 13.5 billion light-years away.

86 Between 1993 and 2009 Hubble Space Telescope (HST) has been serviced five times by astronauts for items such as batteries, gyroscopes, and electronic boxes, and to install new-age science instruments.

87 One of the most stunning images clicked by HST is "Pillars of Creation". The three columns of cosmic dust and gas in the image are part of an active star forming region within the Eagle Nebula.

88 Some of the amazing HST discoveries are: distribution of dark matter in the universe, five moons of Pluto, the collision of comet Shoemaker Levy-9 with Jupiter, the existence of black holes in every galaxy, alien worlds, and the age of the universe.

Collision of comet Shoemaker Levy-9 with Jupiter

89 Hubble transmits about 150 gigabits of raw science data every week. It has made more than 1.5 million observations since its mission began in 1990.

James Webb Telescope

90 NASA's James Webb Space Telescope (JWST), an infrared space observatory, was launched on Dec 25, 2021, from the launch site at Kourou in French Guiana aboard an Ariane 5 rocket. Recognised as a successor to Hubble Space Telescope, it is NASA's largest and most powerful space science telescope.

91 James Webb is about 100 times more powerful than the Hubble Telescope. The diameter of its primary mirror is 6.5 metres and that of its secondary mirror is only 0.74 metres. The telescope orbits the Sun nearly 1.5 billion kilometres from Earth.

92 JWST takes pictures mostly in infrared. With infrared, Webb will be able to capture extremely old galaxies that are currently being pushed farther away from Earth and becoming redder.

93 The first quality science image, revealed on July 11, 2022, by JWST, shows the deepest infrared view of the universe to date. The 13.5-billion-year-old galaxy was spotted in this deep field image captured by Webb.

94 The science goals of JWST are: to know more about the early stages of the universe after the Big Bang, to understand the evolution of galaxies and to study what happened after the first stars were formed, to use infrared probing inside the clouds of gases, and to find other planetary systems and origins of life.

95 Webb clicked a composite image of a cosmic cliff in Carina Nebula which is a massive cloud of dust and gas located 7,500 light-years away from Earth.

96 The James Webb Space Telescope (JWST) was first known as the Next Generation Space Telescope until being renamed in September 2002 in honour of James Edwin Webb, a former NASA administrator who led the organisation from 1961 to 1968.

97 It has found signs of water, along with indications of clouds and haze, in the atmosphere of a giant gas planet WASP 96-b, 1,150 light-years away from Earth, orbiting a sun-like star.

98 Stephan's Quintet is a group of five nearby galaxies. The clear image captured by Webb will help the scientists to study how stars are formed from dust and gas when such nearby galaxies interact.

Galaxies

99 A galaxy is a vast collection of stars, solar systems, gas, and dust held together by gravity. Astronomers and scientists estimate that there could be 100 billion galaxies in the observable universe.

100 Depending on the shape we observe from Earth, galaxies are classified into four types: spiral galaxies have arms curving out from a central cluster of stars, barred spiral have a straight bar across the centre which joins the spiral arms, elliptical are a simple ball shape, and irregular galaxies do not have a clear shape.

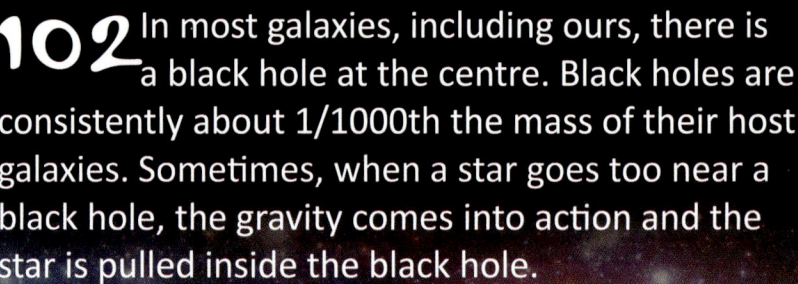

101 Our planet Earth is a member of our solar system. Our solar system is a miniscule part of a large cluster of stars known as the Milky Way galaxy.

102 In most galaxies, including ours, there is a black hole at the centre. Black holes are consistently about 1/1000th the mass of their host galaxies. Sometimes, when a star goes too near a black hole, the gravity comes into action and the star is pulled inside the black hole.

103 Galaxies are mainly empty areas, despite being full of stars. The distance between the stars can vary from 6 to 130,000 kilometres. Stars slowly circle the galactic centre while being kept together by gravity.

104 Some galaxies produce high velocity galactic winds, expelling gas and dust into the intergalactic medium. They are usually observed in galaxies that have a higher rate of star formation than others.

105 The galaxies in the universe are not evenly distributed: most of them are grouped and clustered together, with groups holding up to a few dozen galaxies and clusters containing thousands of galaxies. Superclusters are even bigger structures made up of groups, clusters, and other isolated galaxies.

106 Oftentimes, two galaxies collide and merge into each other. The process takes billions of years. Usually, stars of the merging galaxies do not collide, but gas clouds do. Merging also affects the shape of the galaxies and sometimes creates new stars.

107 The most common type of galaxy in the universe is a dwarf galaxy, but because of their small size, low mass, and low luminosity, they are hard to spot. They are usually found orbiting a larger galaxy in galaxy clusters.

Milky Way Galaxy

108 The Milky Way galaxy is home to the Sun and our solar system. It is a galaxy with millions of stars, their planets, and gas and dust that are all gravitationally bound together. The Milky Way has an estimated 200 billion stars.

109 In the night sky, the Milky Way looks like a milky stripe of light. It was for this reason the ancient Romans called it *"via lacteal"*, which means "way of the milk". It was given a similar name by the ancient Greeks: *"galaxias kylos"*, which translates to "milky circle."

110 The Milky Way is a large barred spiral galaxy in the shape of a disc, with an elliptical bulge of densely packed stars in the centre. It has two major arms, two minor arms and several fragments of arms, called spurs.

111 The Milky Way has a diameter of between 120,000 and 80,000 light-years. About 27,000 light-years from the Galactic Centre, our solar system is located on the inner margin of a minor spiral arm called the Orion spur. Our solar system takes about 240 million years to complete one orbit of the Milky Way.

Our Planet Hunting Neighborhood

Sun → Most of the planets found to date lie within about 300 light-years from our Sun.

112 The centre of the Milky Way is known as the Galactic Centre, where a supermassive black hole, called Sagittarius A*, exists that is equal to around 4 million solar masses.

113 The Canis Major Dwarf galaxy is Milky Way's closest neighbour. This galaxy is about 42,000 light-years away from the galactic centre and only 25,000 light-years away from our solar system. The Sagittarius Dwarf Elliptical galaxy is the next closest, at 70,000 light-years from the Sun.

114 The Crab Nebula is the remnant of an exploded star in the constellation of Taurus. It was discovered by John Bevis, an English astronomer, in 1731.

115 The Local Group is the name of the galaxy group our Milky Way belongs to. Andromeda is the biggest galaxy of this group and Triangulum is third largest after the Milky Way. Andromeda is approaching fast towards our galaxy and in 4.5 billion years both the galaxies are destined to collide with each other.

116 According to recent research, the Milky Way may only be 10 billion years old, not 13.6 billion, as estimated earlier. Different methods, including radioactive dating and observing the stars in the galaxy, are used by scientists to ascertain the age.

Black Holes

117 Using Einstein's general relativity equations, German mathematician Karl Schwarzschild, in 1916, proved the existence of black holes. The term "Black Hole" was coined by theoretical physicist John Wheeler many years later, in 1967.

Karl Schwarzschild

John Wheeler

118 Black holes are regions in space where gravity is so strong that nothing, not even light, can escape them. As they are very dark, they cannot be seen with the naked eye, and can only be detected by space telescopes and other instruments.

119 The smallest black holes in our universe were created at the time of the Big Bang. A stellar black hole is formed when a massive, dying star collapses in on itself. A supermassive black hole is thought to have formed at the same time as its galaxy.

120 Cygnus X-1, the world's first black hole, was discovered in 1964. It is a stellar black hole, around 7,200 light-years away from Earth, with a mass of about 21 times that of our Sun. Its small size makes it quite difficult to image the accretion disc around the event horizon using only radio telescopes.

121 The first image of a black hole was captured in 2019 by the Event Horizon Telescope collaboration. This black hole is at the centre of the M87 galaxy 55 million light-years from Earth. According to NASA, there could be around 10 million to a billion stellar black holes in the Milky Way.

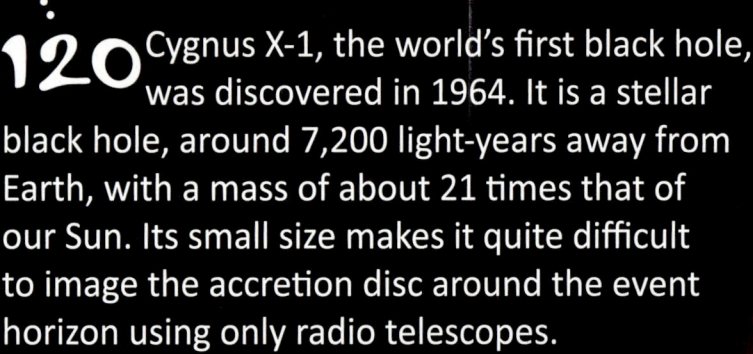

122 The largest black holes are called supermassive. The mass of billions of suns can be found in supermassive black holes. According to astronomers, most galaxies have supermassive black holes at their centres. Sagittarius A*, the star at the centre of our own Milky Way galaxy, is around 4 million times as massive as the Sun.

123 The perimeter of a black hole is its event horizon. It is merely a point in space, past which it is impossible to escape the gravity of the black hole. Objects falling into the black hole cannot leave it once they pass the event horizon.

Accretion Disc
Relativistic Jet
Event Horizon
Singularity

124 It is impossible to know what is inside the black holes as their centre is so dense that everything including light is absorbed by them. According to astrophysical theories the whole mass of a black hole is concentrated at its centre. This single point in spacetime is called singularity.

125 An accretion disc is a band of diffused materials, debris, and gases around the black hole which is in continuous orbital motion. The chaotic motion of the infalling materials heat up the accretion disc, making it emit photon radiations. The electromagnetic radiations of the accretion disc help scientists to know more about the black holes.

Nebulae

126 Nebulae are enormous clouds of gas and dust, primarily hydrogen and helium, as well as other ionised gases that are found in space. They reside in interstellar space, which is the region between stars.

127 Some nebulae (more than one nebula) are made of gas and dust that have been released from the explosion of a collapsing star called a supernova. Other nebulae are areas where new star formation takes place. Our Sun and planets formed in the solar nebula about 4.5 billion years ago.

128 The Helix Nebula is the closest nebula to Earth and is approximately 700 light-years away from it. This nebula is the remains of a dying star, much like our Sun.

129 Our galaxy, the Milky Way, has many nebulae. They are largely found near the centre of the galaxy. Nebulae are also found in other galaxies. Space telescopes such as Spitzer, Hubble and Webb have captured many images of distant nebulae.

130 Stars form in the nebula when gravity starts pulling the clumps of gas and dust together. As the clumps grow in size, their gravity also increases. Finally, the clump collapses under its own gravity causing the core to heat up and begin the star formation.

131 HII regions and dark nebulae are where stars are born. They are primarily composed of hydrogen and helium with small percentages of other gases. Supernova remnants are the remains of massive dying stars. There are neutron stars or possibly black holes present in these expanding clouds of gas and dust.

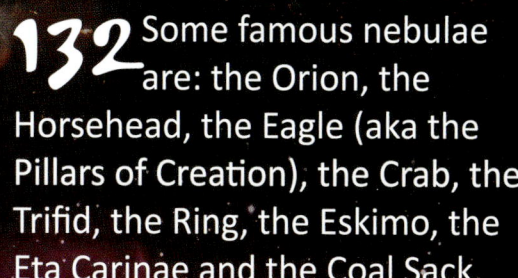

132 Some famous nebulae are: the Orion, the Horsehead, the Eagle (aka the Pillars of Creation), the Crab, the Trifid, the Ring, the Eskimo, the Eta Carinae and the Coal Sack.

133 A "Planetary Nebula" is the last stage in the life of a star that is large and low mass, like the Sun. An "Emission Nebula" emits radiation due to high temperature gas. This causes the nebula to glow. A "Reflection Nebula" reflects the light energy from a nearby star.

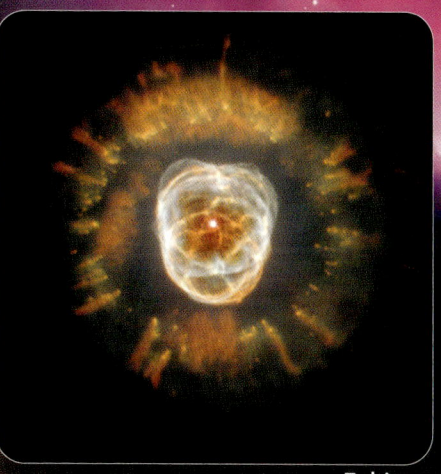

Horsehead

Eskimo

134 The Orion Nebula is one of the most famous and brightest nebulae that is visible to the naked eye. Located in the Milky Way, it is a diffuse nebula that also goes by the name Messier 42 or M42.

500 Fantastic Facts

Pulsars

135 Pulsars are a kind of neutron star that form when a large, massive star reaches the end of its life and explodes in a bright burst called a supernova. The inner core of such a star collapses under gravity and may become either a black hole or a neutron star.

136 Pulsars have strong magnetic fields that are a trillion times stronger than Earth's. Magnetic fields of some pulsars produce bright gamma ray radiations. Astronomers detect pulsars by the periodic radio waves that they emit.

137 Pulsars were first discovered in 1967 by Professor Jocelyn Bell Burnell. A pulsar is a combination of the words "pulsating" and "quasar."

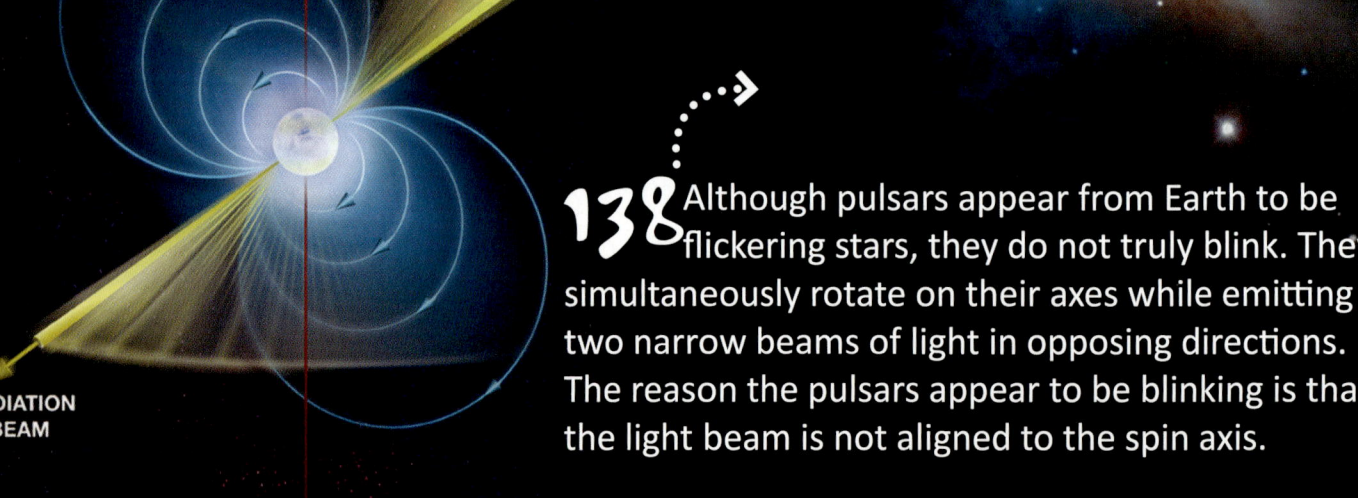

138 Although pulsars appear from Earth to be flickering stars, they do not truly blink. They simultaneously rotate on their axes while emitting two narrow beams of light in opposing directions. The reason the pulsars appear to be blinking is that the light beam is not aligned to the spin axis.

139 Pulsars are rotating at immense speed. Slow pulsars rotate once per second while millisecond pulsars (MSP) rotate hundreds of times per second. The fastest known millisecond pulsars can rotate more than 700 times per second.

140 The discovery of extrasolar planets in orbit, detection of gravitational waves and exploration of interstellar medium have all been made possible because of pulsars. The first extrasolar planets were found because of the 1992 discovery of the Pulsar, PSR B1257+12.

141 Astronomers currently recognise three distinct classes of pulsars based on the source of electromagnetic radiation. These are rotation-powered pulsars, accretion-powered pulsars, and magnetars.

142 A pulsar has the highest energy and fastest rotating speed when it first forms. Constant discharge of electromagnetic energy through its beams gradually slows it down. The beams turn off completely in 110—100 million years and the pulsar goes silent.

Star: Birth

143 Since the beginning of time, stars have been forming throughout the universe. They form in huge clouds and serve as the foundation for galaxies. Astronomers estimate that there are roughly 300 billion stars in our Milky Way galaxy alone.

144 Stars are born inside cold, dense clouds of hydrogen-rich gas and dust. A trigger, such as a shockwave from a supernova explosion or a collision with another cloud, starts the process of star creation.

145 The trigger makes the cloud unstable, and it breaks up into fragments. The materials inside the fragments are pulled by their own gravity into tighter clumps. As the clumps shrink they slowly turn into a sphere and finally become a protostar.

146 Gravity draws material into the protostar's core, building up its temperature, pressure, and density. The material being drawn in begins to spin, sending forth strong gas jets from the centre. Nuclear reactions begin when the pressure and temperature reach a certain level, and the star starts to shine.

147 Stars typically form in clusters at around the same time from the same cloud of matter. Over time, the stars in a cluster separate and either exist alone in space, like our Sun, or occasionally with another star.

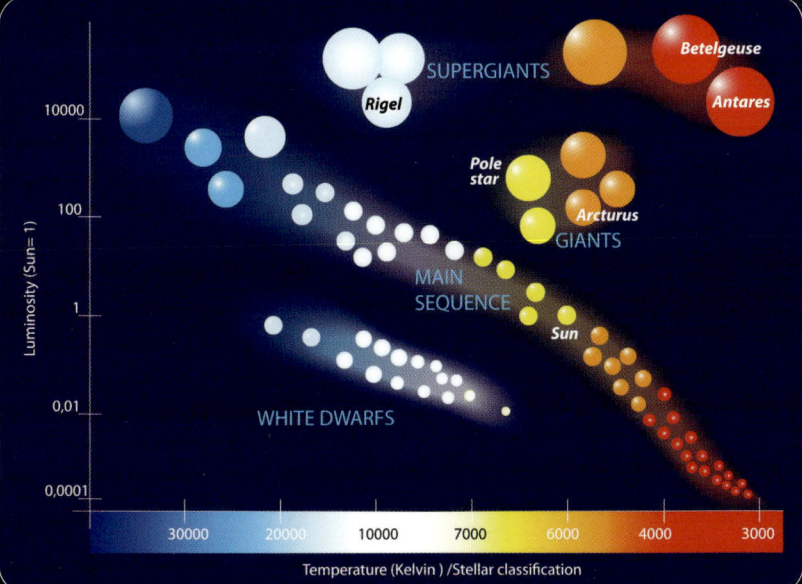

148 The brightness of a star depends upon its luminosity (release of energy) and its distance from Earth. The fact that different stars have different surface temperatures also affects colour. Cooler stars appear to have orange or red hues, whereas hot stars appear white or blue. The Hertzsprung-Russell diagram is used by astronomers to categorise stars by plotting their temperature against luminosity.

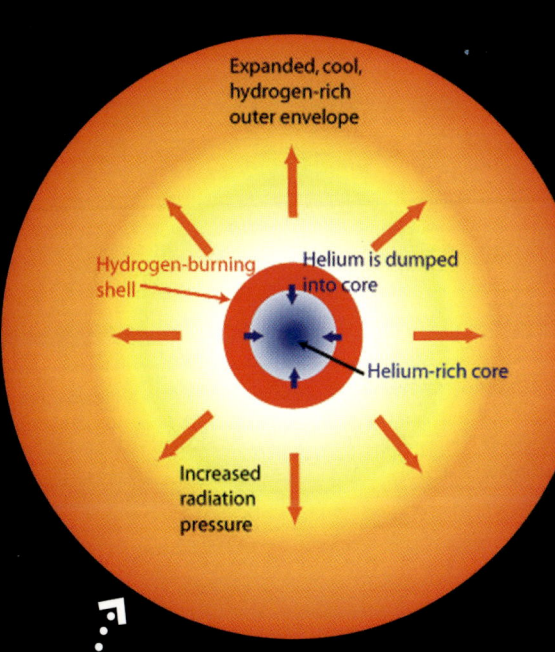

150 Towards the end of its life, when a main sequence star's hydrogen fuel for nuclear fusion is exhausted, the hot core pushes the outer layer outward. It causes the star to swell up and change into a red giant and then shrink to become a white dwarf.

149 Most of the stars in our galaxy, including our Sun, are all main sequence stars. These stars are experiencing nuclear reactions in their core where hydrogen is being converted into helium and releasing a huge amount of energy in the process.

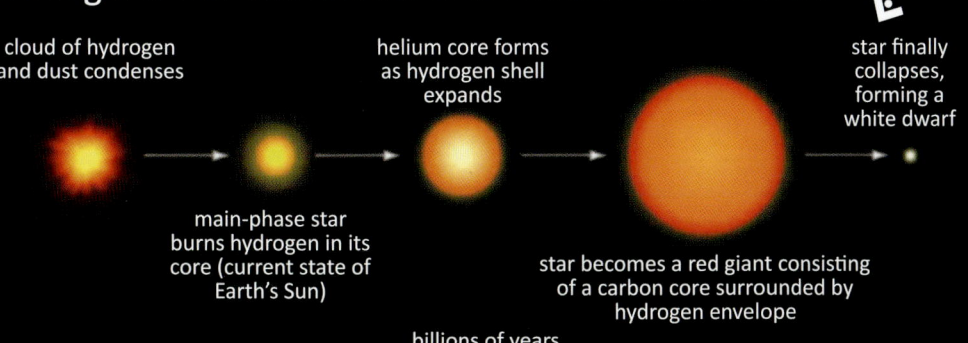

Star: Death

151 All stars eventually use up their fuel and come to an end. The mass of a star and the force with which its core is compressed by gravity determines how it dies. Most stars have enough fuel to last billions of years.

152 In small stars, when hydrogen in the core is exhausted, the star's light gradually dims. When larger stars (8—10 times the mass of Sun) run out of fuel, they swell into red supergiants. They continue to exist for a few million years in this state before exploding luminously and violently – a supernova.

153 When a sun-like star has used up all of its hydrogen fuel, it expands to become a red giant. It becomes big enough to swallow the nearby planets. The core becomes hot and dense enough to cause the helium to fuse into carbon.

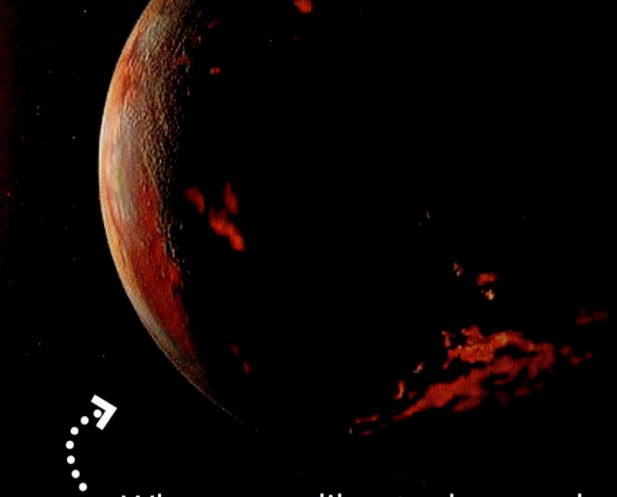

154 The star blows off its outer layer as it runs out of helium. The debris from the outer layer gathers around the dying star to form a planetary nebula. The core shrinks further and becomes a white dwarf and then eventually a black dwarf.

155 The death of a massive star (over eight times our sun) is always violent. Near the end of their lives, they start fusing not only hydrogen and helium but also some heavier elements such as carbon, oxygen, and magnesium. The star swells into a supergiant. The formation of the iron core stops generating outward pressure, and the star collapses causing a supernova blast.

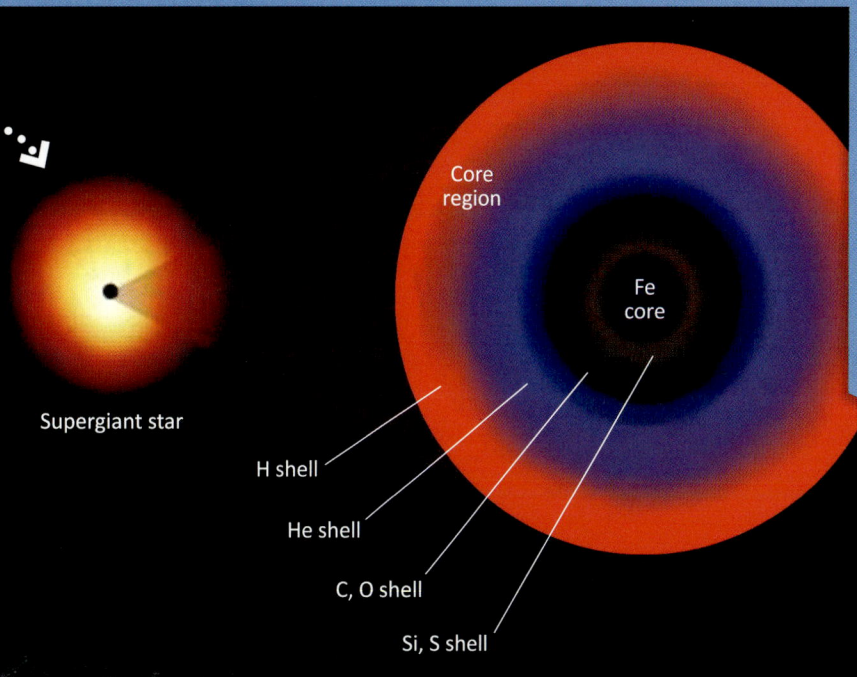

Supergiant star

Core region
Fe core
H shell
He shell
C, O shell
Si, S shell

156 For a week or so, the supernova outshines all of the other stars in its galaxy. Then it quickly fades. All that is left is a tiny, dense object — a neutron star or a black hole — surrounded by an expanding cloud of very hot gas.

157 Upon a star's death, all the elements that made up its core are scattered into space to become components of interstellar clouds of gas and dust. These chemical components serve as the building blocks for future generations of planets, stars, and life.

158 For the first time in history, scientists in Hawaii were able to observe the death of a red supergiant in 2022. They observed the star during its last 130 days, leading up to its self-destruction and the final collapse into a Type II supernova.

Formation of the Solar System

159 The solar system is thought to have formed 4.6 billion years ago from a dense cloud of gases and dust that may have resulted from the shockwave caused by the explosion of a nearby star (supernova).

160 The cloud of dust collapsed into a spinning, rotating disc of gases, called solar nebula. Material began to accumulate in the centre due to gravity. At some point, due to high pressure, the hydrogen atoms started to combine to produce helium.

161 The process released a huge amount of energy, and our Sun was born. Through time, it accumulated more than 99 percent of the accessible material. The left-over material also clumped together to form planets, dwarf planets, and moons.

162 In the initial stages of its formation the Sun was a protosun, having a thin mass. Over millions of years, through the addition of gases from the surrounding nebula, the mass increased. The protosun continued to contract under its own gravity and grew hotter, developing first into a young star and eventually into our Sun.

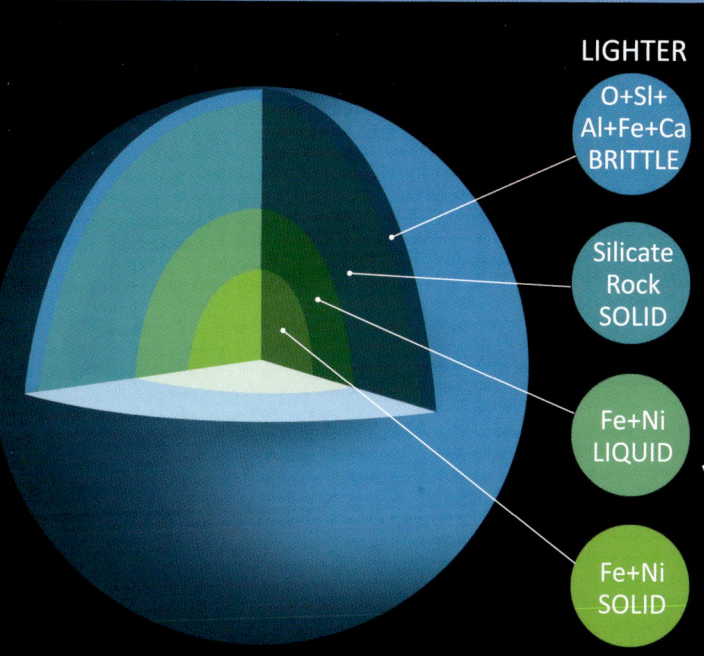

163 The process by which various particles hit and cluster together to create larger masses that can subsequently give rise to planets is known as core accretion. A planet of this type often accumulates its heavy elements near its core and its lighter elements on the surface.

164 A planetesimal is a small celestial body that formed from dust, rock, and other materials floating in the protoplanetary disc. These planetesimals collided, coalesced, and grew into larger objects known as protoplanets, which were predecessors of the current planets of our solar system.

165 During the early stages, the inner solar system's temperature measured nearly 1,700°C while the outer solar system was merely -220°C.

166 At the beginning of the solar system, only rocky materials could withstand the heat of the Sun. For this reason, the first four planets closest to the Sun are all terrestrial. In the outer solar system, gases condensed to form gas and ice giants.

167 The matter in the disc did not always clump together to form planets or moons. Jupiter is the bits and pieces of the early solar system that never fully formed into planets.

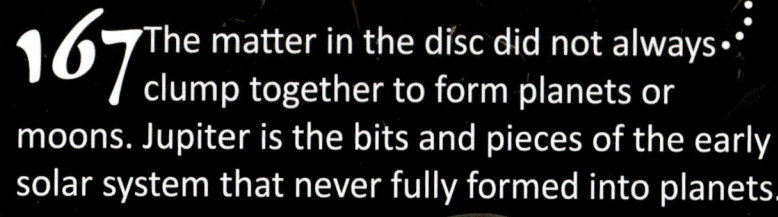

Constituents of the Solar System

168 The solar system consists of a central star – the Sun – along with eight planets, numerous dwarf planets, more than 100 moons, countless millions of asteroids, comets, and meteoroids.

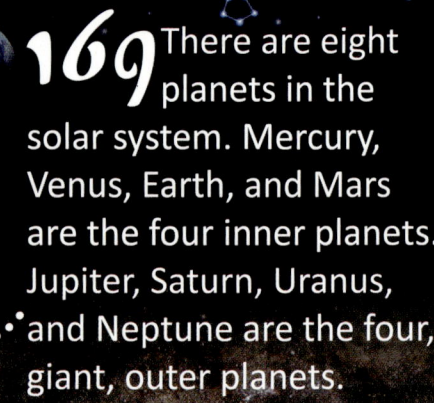

169 There are eight planets in the solar system. Mercury, Venus, Earth, and Mars are the four inner planets. Jupiter, Saturn, Uranus, and Neptune are the four, giant, outer planets.

170 Asteroids are giant space rocks that float around the inner solar system. Most of the asteroids in the solar system are found in the asteroid belt between Mars and Jupiter, but some occasionally come dangerously close to Earth. Their size ranges from a few metres to about 1,000 kilometres and they are also known as planetoids or minor planets.

171 Comets are small ice bodies of frozen gases, rocks and dust that orbit the Sun. When a comet approaches the Sun, it heats up and begins to release dust and gases which look like a long, bright tail in the sky.

172 Meteoroids are small rocky objects, often a small piece of an asteroid or a comet, in outer space that usually range in size from a few millimetres to smaller than a kilometre. A meteor will become visible to the naked eye between 77 and 119 kilometres above the Earth's surface. The Hoba meteorite, weighing 60,000 kg and measuring 2.7 m by 2.4 m, is the largest meteorite found on Earth.

173 Oort Cloud is a spherical shaped region surrounding the Sun, far beyond the orbits of the outermost planets. It contains trillions of icy bodies and is over one light-year away from the Sun. It is believed to be the home of long-period comets.

174 According to the IAU a planet should orbit a star, it should be spherical in shape, and it should not share its orbit with an object of a similar size. A dwarf planet is an astronomical body that satisfies the first two criteria but not the last one. For this reason, Pluto is now classified as a dwarf planet.

175 Th Kuiper Belt is a disc-shaped region outside the orbit of Neptune. It contains hundreds of millions of small ice bodies, comets, and dwarf planets. Pluto, Eris, Makemake and Haumea are some of the most famous Kuiper Belt Objects (KBO).

The Sun 1

176 Our Sun is a medium-sized yellow dwarf star that is 4.3 billion years old and has the potential to last up to 7 billion years longer. It will ultimately become a white dwarf and lose most of its mass and heat.

177 The Sun contains 99.8 percent of all the matter in the solar system. Slightly bigger than a typical star, the Sun is about 1.392 million kilometres in diameter, which is about 109 times broader than our Earth. It has a volume large enough to swallow 1.3 million Earths.

178 Hydrogen and helium make up the majority of the Sun's composition, with 75 percent and 24 percent respectively. Trace quantities of other elements such as lithium, beryllium, boron, iron, nickel, calcium, sodium, magnesium, and uranium are also present.

Hydrogen 75 %
Helium 24 %
Oxygen, Carbon, Nitrogen, Neon, Silicon, Iron

150 million kilometres

179 The distance of the Sun from Earth is 150 million kilometres. Sunlight takes 8 minutes and 19 seconds to reach Earth. The Sun is more than 333,000 times bigger than Earth.

180 Nuclear fusion is the process through which the Sun produces energy. It is a continuous process where under intense temperature and pressure hydrogen is fusing to form helium. The fusion releases gigantic amounts of energy – in the range of 4.26 million metric tonnes per second.

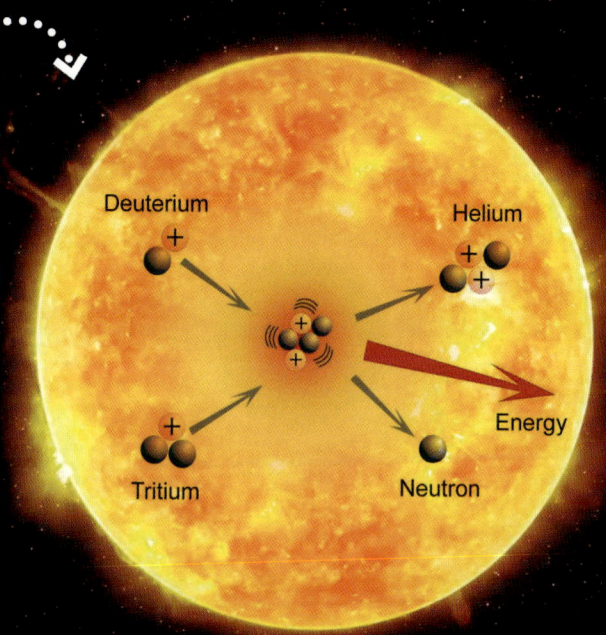

181 The Sun has an extremely strong magnetic field because it is an electrically charged ball of gas. The solar cycle, which lasts around 11 years, is a full cycle of this magnetic field. The magnetic fields of the Sun entirely reverse at the end of each cycle.

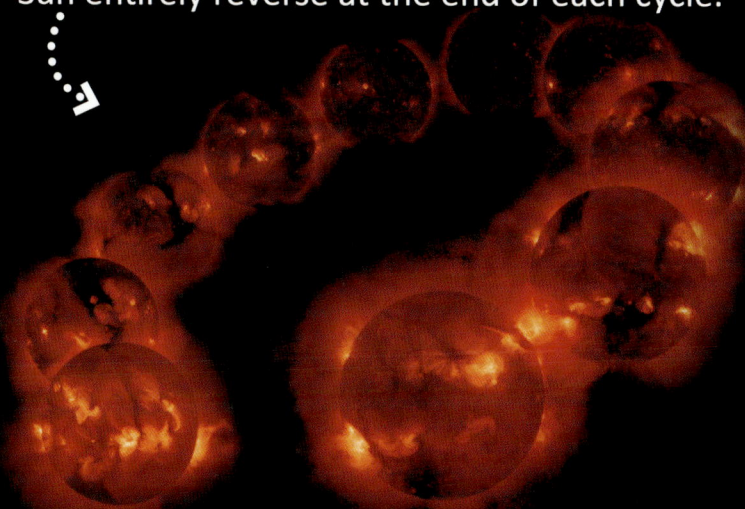

182 Like Earth, the Sun rotates anti-clockwise around its own axis. A single rotation of the Sun takes between 25 (at the equator) and 34 days (at the poles). The Sun revolves around the Milky Way in a clockwise direction. One complete orbit of the Sun around the galactic centre takes between 225 and 250 million years.

183 A torrent of extremely hot, charged particles known as the solar wind is ejected from the Sun's upper atmosphere. It blows for around 10 billion kilometres with a great speed. Sometimes the particles of the wind enter Earth's atmosphere and create brilliant auroras in the polar skies.

184 A coronal mass ejection (CME) is the expulsion of a huge cloud of superhot, electrically charged particles from the Sun's corona. Geomagnetic storms can occur when CMEs arrive near Earth. They also affect electric grids, the internet, and satellite communication systems.

The Sun 2

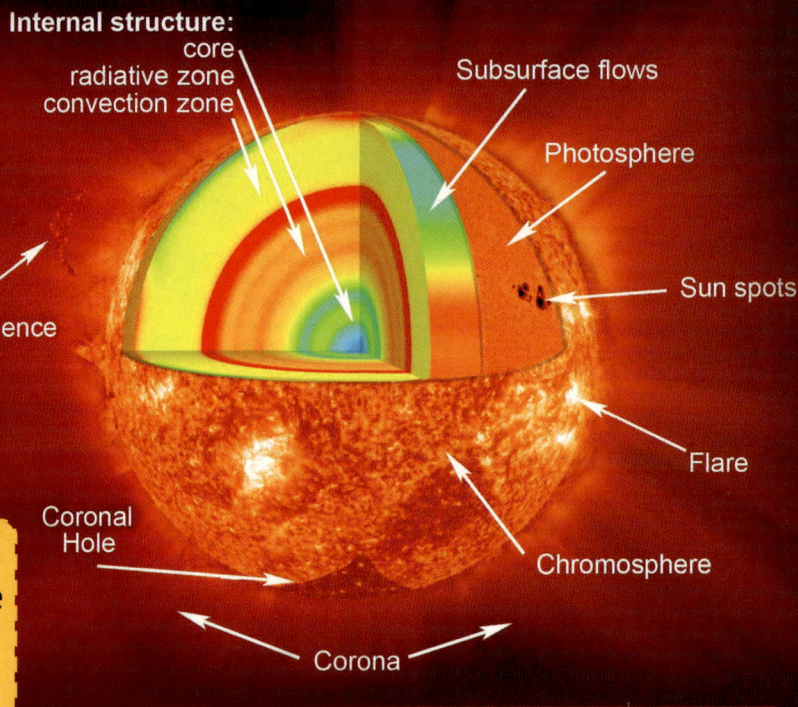

Internal structure: core, radiative zone, convection zone — Subsurface flows, Photosphere, Sun spots, Flare, Chromosphere, Corona, Coronal Hole, Prominence

185 There are seven separate layers to the Sun. Core, radiative zone, and convection zone make up the inner layers. The outermost layers include the photosphere, chromosphere, transition zone, and corona.

186 With a temperature of 15 million degrees Celsius the "core" is the hottest and densest layer. About 600 million tonnes of hydrogen are fused into helium per second in a continuous process of nuclear fusion.

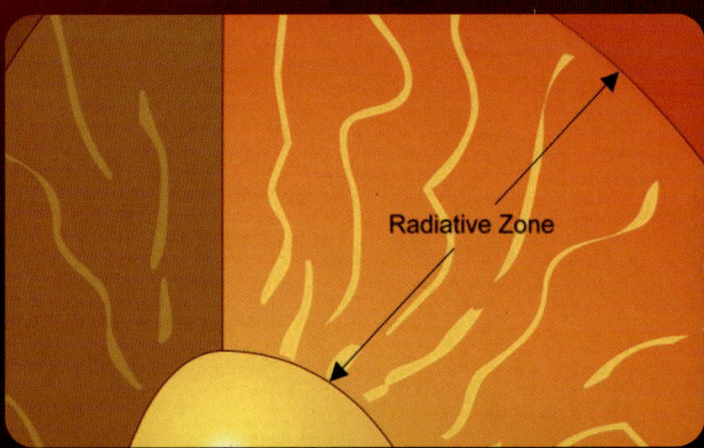

Convective Zone, Radiative Zone, Core

187 Exterior to the core is the "radiative" zone which is less dense than the core. No nuclear fusion takes place in this layer. Energy produced in the core slowly moves out through this layer as electromagnetic radiation.

188 "Convection" zone is the outermost layer of the Sun's interior zones. Energy is transported to Sun's exterior from the interior by convection.

189 The visible, brightly yellow surface of the sun is known as the "photosphere". Temperatures in the photosphere, which is around 400 kilometres thick, can get as high as 5,700°C. The thermal columns of the convection zone make it look granular. The photosphere is where sunspots, solar flares, and solar prominences take form.

190 "Chromosphere" is a 2,000-kilometre-thick, pinkish red layer that is filled with jets of hot gas. It frequently emits torrents of burning gases called spicules that give a hair-like appearance around a sunspot. Spicules last for just 15 minutes.

191 The Sun's outermost layer, the "corona", begins approximately 2,100 km above the photosphere. The corona has a temperature of at least 500,000°C. The corona cannot be seen with the naked eye except during a total solar eclipse.

192 The first spacecraft to study the Sun, Solrad 1, was launched by the United States in 1960. Since then, various missions have been launched to gather data and study the Sun, including the Solar and Heliospheric Observatory (SOHO) and Voyager 1 and 2.

193 Isaac Newton used a telescope and prism to prove that sunlight was actually a spectrum of colours. The invention of an optical instrument called spectroscope, in 1860, made it possible to distinguish between the many wavelengths of visible light and other electromagnetic waves.

Meteoroids

194 Meteoroids are chunks of rock and iron that orbit the Sun. A meteoroid's composition and dimension determines the length of its light trail. Millions of meteoroids impact Earth's atmosphere every day. The fastest meteoroids can travel up to 94,000 miles per hour.

195 Numerous meteoroids are broken-up pieces of asteroids that collided in the asteroid belt between the paths of Mars and Jupiter. The power of the asteroid impact can force the asteroids, as well as the meteoroid debris, out of their normal orbits.

196 A small portion of meteoroids are rocky fragments that splinter off when asteroids or meteoroids collide with a planet or a moon. The impact creates craters on the surface of the celestial body and more debris is thrown back into the solar system.

197 Most meteoroids are composed of heavier metals such as nickel and iron as well as the silicate minerals. While stony meteoroids are small and brittle, metal meteoroids are large and dense. A total of more than 50,000 meteorites have been found on Earth, 99.8 percent of which are from asteroids and the rest from Mars and the Moon.

198 Some meteoroids are debris thrown out by comets as they fly through space. Thousands or perhaps hundreds of meteoroids and micrometeoroids could be present in the dusty tail of the comet.

199 A meteoroid, when passed through the planet's atmosphere, typically burns up (due to friction) and appears as a dash of light, at which point it is referred to as a "meteor" or "shooting star." Sometimes, the meteoroid does not burn completely and falls as a solid piece of debris. This piece is called a "meteorite".

200 An increase in the quantity of meteors that blaze over the night sky is known as a meteor shower. A meteor shower happens when Earth's atmosphere collides with the cometary debris. Very strong meteor showers that produce 1,000 meteors per hour are called meteor storms.

201 Though harmless, meteoroids occasionally present a threat to our spacecrafts. A meteor stream in 1967 damaged the Mariner 4 spacecraft's thermal insulation. The "Persied" meteor shower struck the electronics compartment of Olympus-1 (ESA), 1993.

202 The study of meteorites helps scientists to know about the age and composition of different celestial bodies such as asteroids, comets, moons and even planets. We also learn about the early conditions and mechanisms in the solar system history.

Comets

203 Comets are ice, dust and rock-bearing bodies that circle the Sun in an extremely elliptical path. A comet's distinctive tail is caused by gas and dust released by it as it approaches the Sun. Depending on whether a comet contains more ice material or rocky debris, scientists may call it dirty snowball or snowy dirtball.

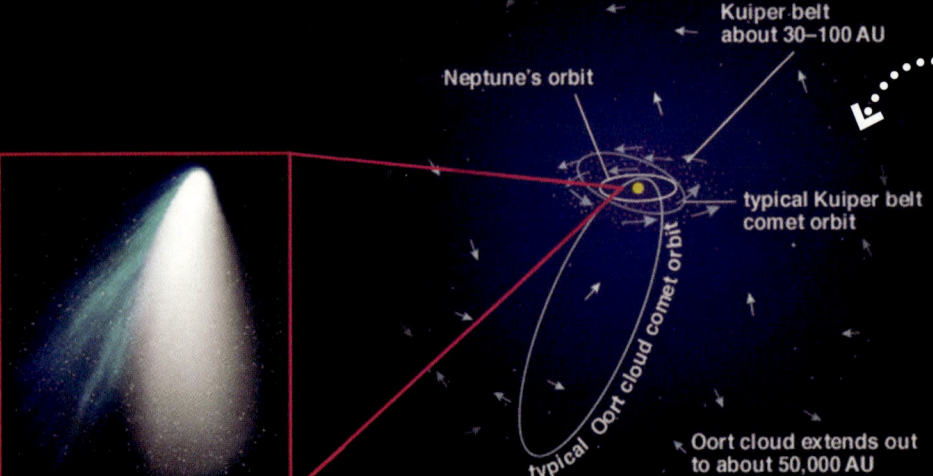

204 NASA reports that as of September 2021, there are 3,743 known comets. The Kuiper Belt is the origin point of short-period comets. Even further out, the nearly spherical Oort Cloud is thought to be the source of long-period comets.

205 "Short-period" comets take 200 years or less to complete one orbit around the Sun, "long-period" comets take more than 200 years and "single-apparition" comets leave the solar system after one pass of the Sun.

206 Halley's comet, discovered by the English astronomer, Edmond Halley, is possibly the most famous comet in history. It is a "periodic" comet that visits the area around Earth once every 75 to 76 years.

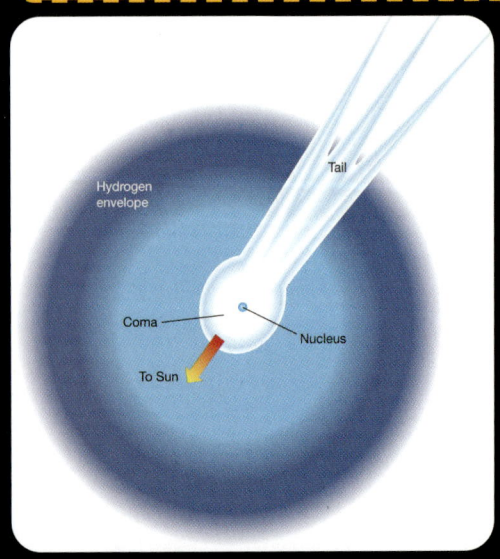

207 The "nucleus" is the solid core of a comet. Its constituents are dust, rock, water, ice and frozen elements. When a comet gets closer to the Sun, the ice on its surface turns into gas, forming a "coma". A coma is 1,000 times larger than the nucleus.

208 A huge "hydrogen envelope" (about 10 km) surrounds the coma, which gets bigger as the comet approaches the Sun. Dust and gas are the two main types of comet tails. Since gas is more strongly affected by solar winds than dust, "Gas Tail" points directly away from the Sun, while "Dust Tail" has a slight curve.

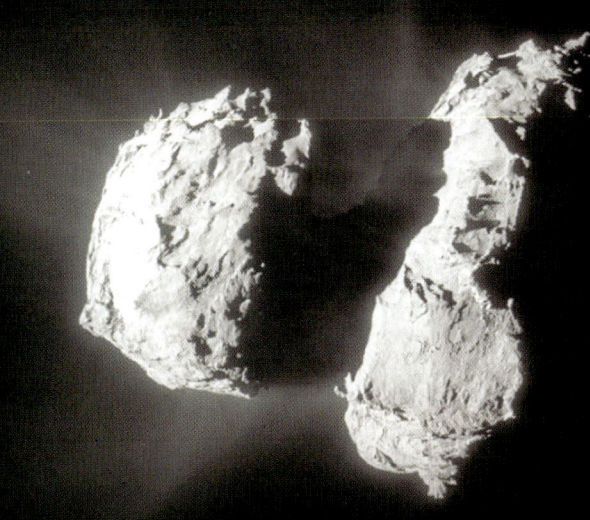

209 The significant likelihood that water and organic molecules were transported to young Earth by asteroids and comets has been the subject of debate among scientists. Now, the Rosetta probe (ESA) has directly discovered glycine in the coma of comet 67P. This amino acid is a vital component of life.

210 The main spacecraft of NASA's Deep Impact mission deployed an impactor into the path of the comet *Tempel 1* on July 2, 2005 and captured the stunning explosion that revealed the internal constitution and structure of its nucleus. In samples returned by NASA's Stardust spacecraft, scientists found glycine, a fundamental building block of life.

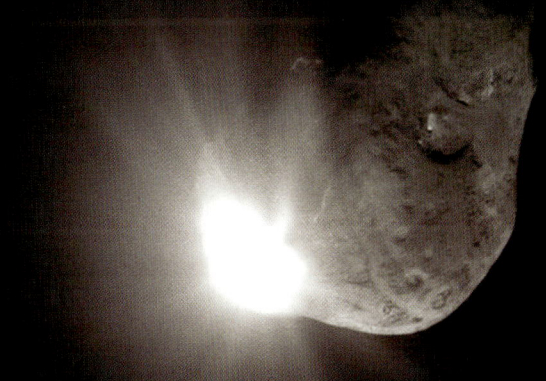

211 Astronomers Pedro Bernardinelli and Gary Bernstein discovered one of the largest known comets to date. The megacomet, named after its discoverers and also known by *C/2014 UN271*, has a diameter of around 120 kilometres and a mass that is roughly estimated to be 450 quadrillion kilos. It is approaching the Sun and will be nearest to it in 2031.

Bernardinelli-Bernstein (C/2014 UN271)

Asteroid

212 Asteroids are small solid bodies that revolve around the Sun along with the planets. They are called minor planets or planetoids because they do not fit the criteria for being termed a planet. They are rocky and metallic bodies of irregular shape with no atmosphere.

213 The C-type (chondrite) asteroids have silicate and clay rocks and are most common. The S-type (stone) are made up of silicate and nickel-iron and the M-type are completely metallic asteroids having nickel-iron.

Chondritic Stony Meteorite — Asteroid Type C

Iron Meteorite — Asteroid Type M

Pallasite Meteorite

Achondritic Stony Meteorite — Asteroid Type S

214 Asteroids are rocky leftovers from the early stages of the solar system's creation, which took place roughly 4.6 billion years ago. The creation of planets followed the formation of the Sun. The objects that failed to form planets collided with each other and broke apart to form the asteroids we see today.

215 Asteroids have different locations in the solar system. The majority of asteroids are found in the main "asteroid belt". "Trojans" share their orbit with a larger planet and are found outside the main belt. The orbits of "Near-Earth Asteroids" (NEAs) pass close to the orbit of Earth and the "centaurs" stay within the bounds of the outer solar system.

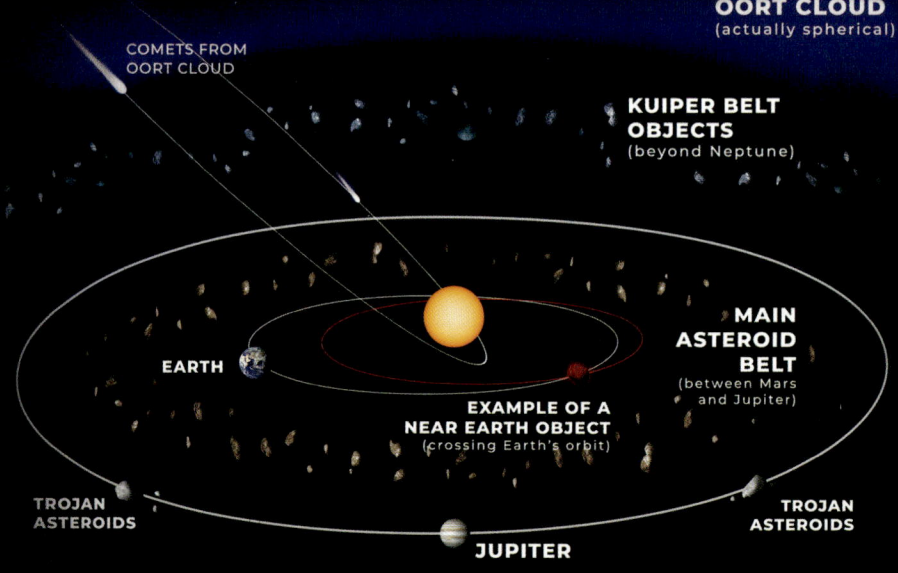

216 Vesta, the second largest asteroid body, is the only asteroid that can be seen with the naked eye because of its reflective surface. It was discovered by the German astronomer Heinrich Wilhelm Matthias Olbers on March 29, 1807.

217 To date, more than 1 million asteroids have been identified by scientists. The size of the asteroids range from 1 metre to 1,000 kilometres and the combined mass of all asteroids is less than Earth's Moon. Asteroids can pose a threat despite their small size.

218 In 1801, Italian astronomer Giuseppe Piazzi discovered Ceres, the first member of the asteroid belt. It is the biggest body in the asteroid belt. Initially called an asteroid it is now regarded as a dwarf planet as it is spherical and revolves around the Sun.

219 Asteroids orbit the sun in elliptical orbits, rotating and sometimes tumbling quite strangely. Many asteroids have one or two tiny partner moons. There are also binary or double asteroid systems, in which two asteroids of nearly identical size orbit one another.

220 To help the world's space agencies in determining how to prevent potentially fatal asteroids from striking Earth, NASA launched the Double Asteroid Redirection Test (DART) in November 2021. The mission aims to test a method of planetary defence against Near-Earth objects (NEOs).

Asteroid Belt

221 Most of the asteroids in the solar system are found in the area between Mars and Jupiter known as the asteroid belt, which also serves as a dividing line between the inner rocky planets and the outer gas giants. To differentiate it from the Kuiper belt, it is sometimes referred to as the main asteroid belt.

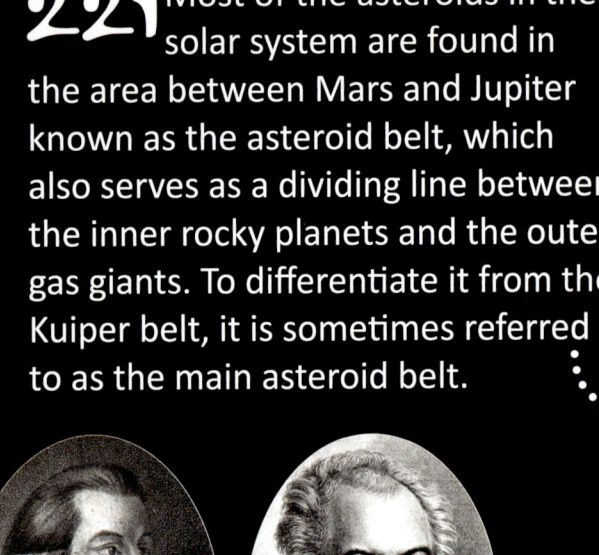

Baron Franz Xaver von Zach

Heinrich Olbers

222 The Titus-Bode Law (1772) indicated a missing planet between Mars and Jupiter. An astronomer group (celestial police) was formed in 1800 to search for the lost planet. Ceres was discovered on January 1, 1801, by astronomer Giuseppe Piazzi. Pallas, Vesta, and Juno were discovered in the coming years. As more of these rocks were found, scientists started referring to them as asteroids and their location as the asteroid belt.

Johann Schröter

Karl Ludwig Harding

223 Astronomer Heinrich Wilhelm Matthias Olbers proposed that the asteroid belt was the result of the disintegration of a huge planet. He called this imaginary planet *Phaeton*. Many astronomers from all over the world agreed with the "disrupted planet hypothesis," which persisted until the end of the 20th century.

224 The asteroid belt's total mass is around 4 percent of the mass of our Moon. The four largest asteroids, Ceres, Vesta, Pallas, and Juno, make up around half of its mass. Ceres is now a dwarf planet, making Vesta the largest asteroid in the belt.

Ceres

Vesta

Pallas

Juno

225 Asteroids in the belt are sparsely distributed. About a million kilometres separate two asteroids on average. Spacecraft passing through the asteroid belt therefore have almost no risk of colliding with an asteroid. Kirkwood Gaps are the regions where the asteroids are almost absent because of Jupiter's gravitational effect.

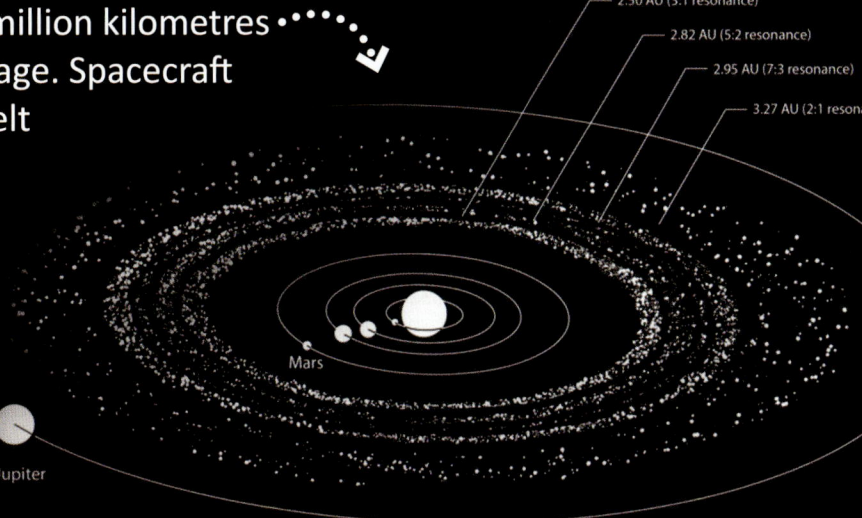

Kirkwood Gaps:
- 2.50 AU (3:1 resonance)
- 2.82 AU (5:2 resonance)
- 2.95 AU (7:3 resonance)
- 3.27 AU (2:1 resonance)

226 In 1972, Pioneer 10 flew through the asteroid belt on its way to Jupiter. In 1989, the Galileo spacecraft examined the asteroids Gaspra and Ida, and discovered Ida's moon Dactyl, the first moon orbiting an asteroid.

227 The Atens, Apollos, and Amors are the three families of Near-Earth Objects (NEA), with Amors never crossing Earth's orbit. The Apollo asteroid 4581 Asclepius (1989 FC), which had a diameter of 300 metres, missed Earth on March 23, 1989, by a distance of 700,000 kilometres. As of June 2021, 26,115 NEAs and 2,185 potentially dangerous asteroids have been detected.

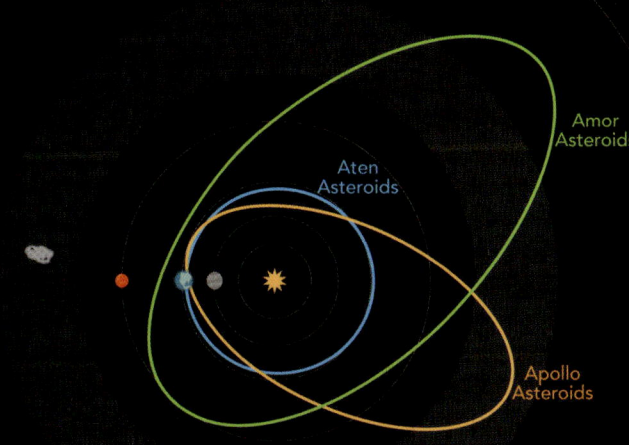

228 According to "Alvarez hypothesis" (Walter and Luis) a huge asteroid crashed into Earth 65 million years ago causing the extinction of dinosaurs. The discovery of a 180-kilometre-wide and 20-kilometre-deep impact crater, called *Chicxulub*, in the Gulf of Mexico, proved the authenticity of the Alvarez hypothesis.

Inner Planets: Terrestrial Planets

229 The planets closest to the Sun are called inner or terrestrial planets. The four inner planets are: Mercury, Venus, Earth, and Mars. The word "terrestrial" comes from the Latin word *"terra"* which means land or Earth. Terrestrial planets are named so because their structure and composition are like those of Earth.

230 All the inner planets formed from the same material around 4.6 billion years ago. A terrestrial planet has a hard, solid surface and is composed mostly of rocks and metals underneath. Early in the history of the solar system, each of these planets was bombarded by comets and asteroids.

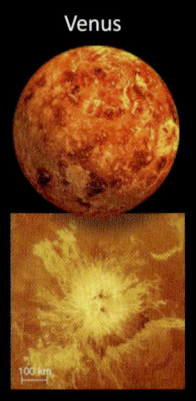

231 As far as the size of terrestrial planets go Earth is the largest, and Venus comes a close second with a size almost similar to Earth. Mars is third, and the smallest among them is Mercury. There may have been more terrestrial planetoids during the solar system's formation, but they either combined or were destroyed.

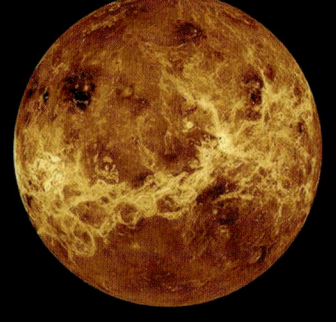

232 There is an atmosphere on every terrestrial planet. Mercury, the smallest planet, has the thinnest, almost negligible atmosphere. Mars has a thin atmosphere as well. The atmosphere of Earth is composed of many layers. Venus has a dense atmosphere that retains heat from the sun.

233 The surface of all terrestrial planets is dominated by common geological features such as canyons, mountains, craters, and volcanoes that are either active or extinct. However, the presence of water varies in all the four planets.

234 Mercury and Venus are the only planets in our solar system with no moons. Their proximity to the Sun could be the reason behind it. The two small moons of Mars, Phobos and Deimos, are irregular in shape. Earth has a single, spherical Moon.

235 Along with the rocky surface, all the terrestrial planets have a core made up of hot, molten metal (mostly iron). The layer above the core is called the mantle and is usually made of silicate rocks. These are rocks rich in silicon and oxygen.

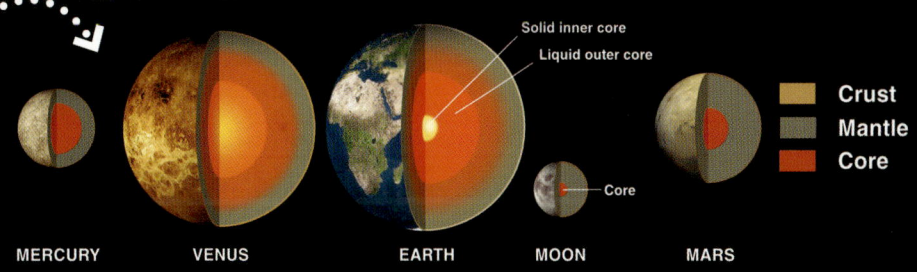

236 There are terrestrial planets around other stars too. According to the Kepler mission data, Earth-sized and so-called "super-Earth" worlds may exist throughout the galaxy. The Milky Way may contain up to 40 billion such exoplanets.

237 Scientists have proposed four categories for classifying terrestrial planets. Silicate planets are the standard type that are seen in the solar system, Iron planets consist almost entirely of iron, Coreless planets have only silicate rock, but no metallic core, and Carbon planets are composed of a metal core surrounded only by carbon based minerals.

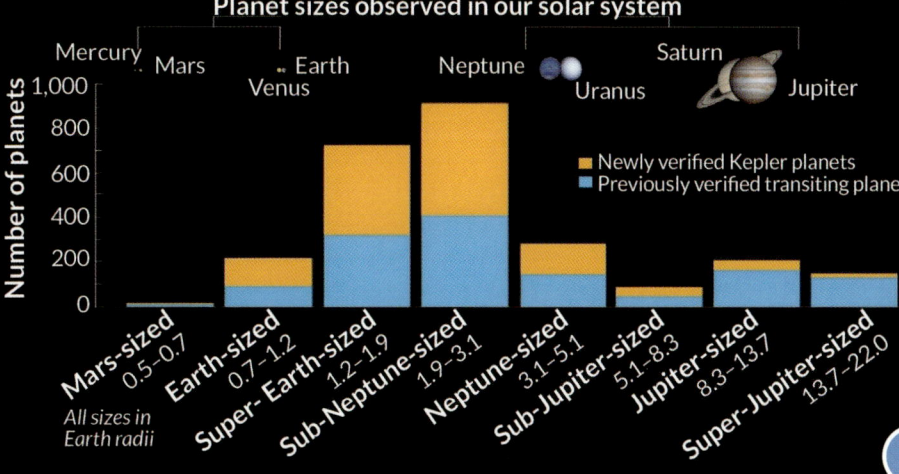

Outer Planets: Gas Giants

238 The four massive planets in the outer solar system are called outer planets or giant planets. Two of these planets, Jupiter and Saturn, fall into the category of gas giants and the other two, Neptune and Uranus, are known as ice giants. Together, these four are also called "Jovian planets", meaning Jupiter like.

Saturn

Jupiter

239 Though the outer planets vary in terms of size, mass, and composition, they all have the same features. They all lack a solid surface and have kept their original, dense atmosphere. They do have large cores, but the metal present is definitely not iron. All the Jovian planets have their own ring systems and a substantial number of moons.

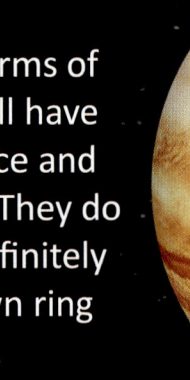

240 Hydrogen and helium are the main components of Jupiter and Saturn, the gas giants. They have layers of molecular hydrogen and liquid metallic hydrogen beneath their heavy atmospheres. They are frequently referred to as "failed stars" because, despite having the same elements that make up a star, they lack the mass to have extremely high pressures and temperatures that would initiate nuclear fusion.

241 James Blish, a science fiction author, first used the term "gas giant" in 1952. At that time, he referred to all the four outer planets. The term is highly inaccurate because at extreme temperature and pressure the matter is above the "critical point" where liquid and vapour can co-exist.

242 Despite being formed of two of the lightest gases (hydrogen and helium) both Jupiter and Saturn can retain a spherical shape. These planets have strong gravitational pull because of their enormous sizes. The spherical shape of gas giants is due to gravity's powerful pull towards the centre.

243 Jupiter is the fifth planet from our Sun and the largest planet in the solar system with its radius almost 11 times the size of Earth. About 1,300 Earths can fit inside it because its volume is more than 1,300 times that of our planet's. It is visible to the naked eye and looks white and shiny in twilight.

244 Saturn is the second largest planet in the solar system, after Jupiter, and the sixth planet from the Sun. The average radius of this gas giant is nine times that of Earth. Due to ammonia crystals in its upper atmosphere, it has a pale-yellow hue. Saturn has 82 moons.

245 Galileo Galilei first identified Jupiter as a planet in 1610, when he used his crude telescope to identify the planet's four largest moons. Prior to that, Jupiter had been seen by Chinese and Babylonian astronomers, but they mistook it for a star.

63

Outer Planets: Ice Giants

246 Uranus and Neptune are two of the furthest planets from the Sun. The term ice giants is used for them because the primary materials they had during their formation was either ice or gas trapped in water ice.

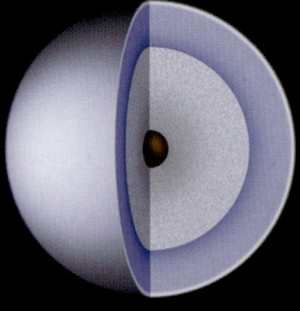
URANUS

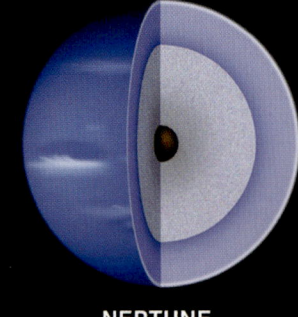
NEPTUNE

- Hydrogen, helium, methane gas
- Mantle (water, ammonia, methane ices)
- Core (rock, ice)

247 The composition of Uranus and Neptune is different from the gas giants. They have higher concentrations of methane and other heavier elements such as oxygen, carbon, nitrogen, and sulphur. Only 20 percent of their composition is hydrogen and helium.

248 The water on ice giants is mostly in the form of a supercritical fluid. The visible clouds are most likely made up of ice crystals with various compositions.

249 The ice giants Uranus and Neptune do not have solid surfaces. Their surfaces are actually layers of gaseous clouds (surrounding a small, solid core), which appear to be solid. Their mantles are a combination of water, ammonia and methane ices, and their cores are a mix of rock and ice.

250 Windstorms can be seen in the upper atmosphere of Neptune because it has the fastest winds in the solar system (1,200 miles per hour). The heat of the core is responsible for this speed. Wind speed in Uranus (560 miles per hour) is less than Neptune's as its core produces less heat.

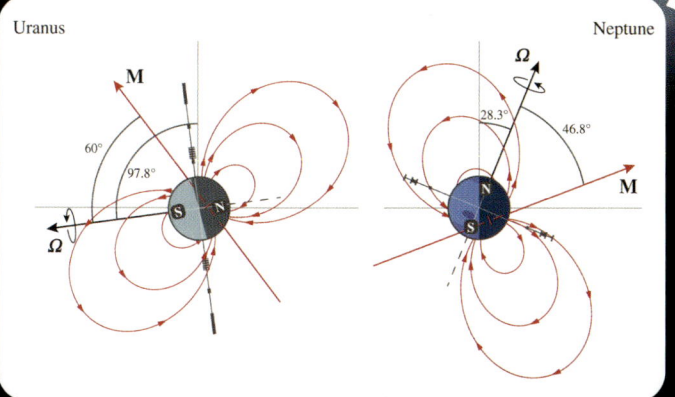

251 In both the ice giants, magnetic fields are offset from their centres and tilted, creating magnetospheres that are asymmetrical in shape. Both the planets have rings and multiple moons.

252 Uranus spins on its side, like a rolling ball. It makes an angle of 97.8° with the plane of its orbit. One complete rotation takes 17 hours and one revolution around the Sun takes 84 Earth years. Neptune's day is 16 hours long and it completes an orbit around the Sun in 165 Earth years.

Uranus orbital tilt: 97.8°

Neptune orbital tilt: 28.3°

253 Due to their excessively low temperatures, Uranus and Neptune can hold condensed methane in their very cold troposphere. The presence of this methane is what gives the ice giants their hazy blue colour.

254 Both the planets have similar atmospheric conditions, but Neptune appears a deeper blue than Uranus. Both planets have a dense haze layer; however, the layer on Uranus is thicker than the layer on Neptune. This concentrated layer of haze is what makes Uranus look lighter blue than Neptune.

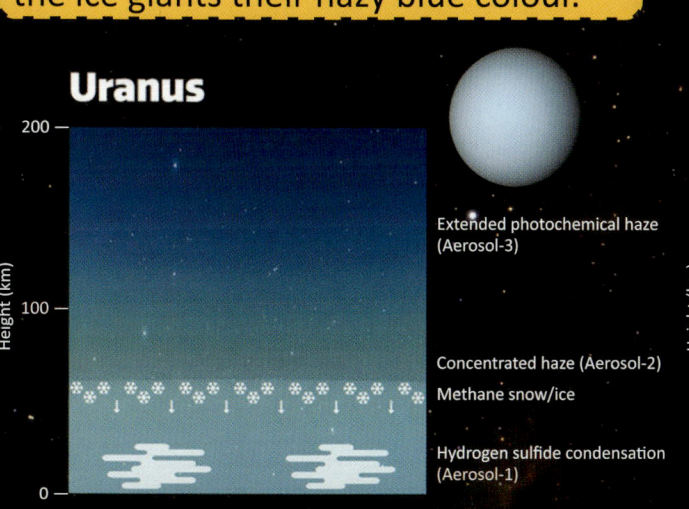

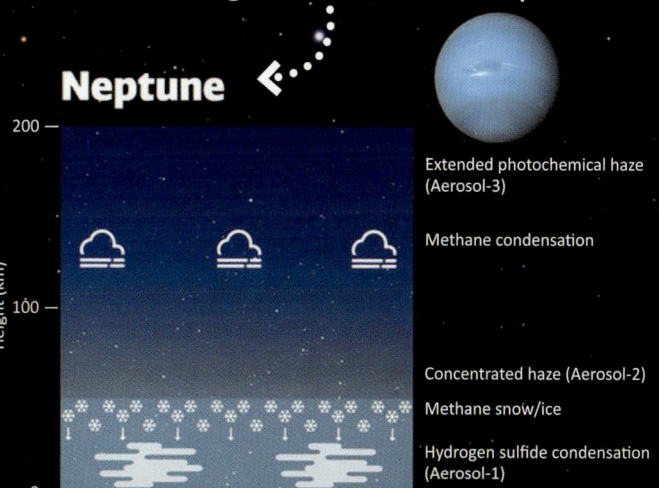

Natural and Artificial Satellites

Ganymeda *Jupiter*   Titan *Saturn*   Callisto *Jupiter*

Io *Jupiter*   Moon *Earth*   Europa *Jupiter*   Triton *Neptune*

255 Natural Satellites are celestial bodies that revolve around a much larger entity. All planets, asteroids and comets orbiting the Sun can be thought of as natural satellites. The objects or the natural satellites orbiting the planets, dwarf planets and other small solar system bodies are simply referred to as "moons".

256 Ganymede, Titan, Callisto, Io, our Moon, Europa, and Triton, are seven of the biggest moons of our solar system. Among these, Ganymede, Callisto, Io, and Europa are moons of Jupiter; Titan orbits Saturn; and Triton is Neptune's moon.

 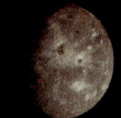   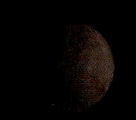

Titania *Uranus*   Rhea *Saturn*   Oberon *Uranus*   Iapetus *Saturn*   Charon *Pluto*   Umbriel *Uranus*

Ariel *Uranus*   Dione *Saturn*   Tethys *Saturn*   Enceladus *Saturn*   Miranda *Uranus*   Proteus *Neptune*   Mimas *Saturn*

257 According to the latest data in the solar system, there are 207 known natural satellites belonging to the six planetary satellite systems. The seven dwarf planets and 442 other minor planets also have their own natural satellites.

258 Galileo Galilei was the first to detect four astronomical bodies orbiting the enormous gas giant Jupiter in 1610. Ganymede, IO, Europa and Callista, the four moons, are now known as Galilean moons.

259 Regular natural satellites have prograde orbits, which means that they orbit in the direction of their planet's motion. Irregular natural satellites orbit against the direction of their planet's rotation, which means they have a retrograde orbit.

Equatorial: i = 0 or 180 Prograde: 0 < i < 90

Polar: i = 90 Retrograde: 90 < i < 180

260 Artificial satellites are manmade satellites that are created to serve a specific purpose. Most of these satellites are launched into an orbit around Earth. There are also some that orbit the Sun, Moon, and other celestial bodies to collect information.

261 Artificial satellites provide a variety of functions, including studying Earth and the other members of the solar system, forecasting weather, aiding in communication, and providing global positioning systems (GPS). They are frequently employed in military operations as information gatherers.

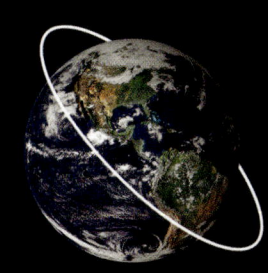

262 CubeSats are small box-shaped satellites (10 cm cube) that are launched into low Earth orbit to survey the planet, try out cutting-edge communications systems, or run miniscule experiments. The most CubeSats ever launched from a single rocket is 120!

263 The non-functional human-made objects left in Earth's orbit or space are called "space junk" or "space debris". Such debris consists of non-operational spacecraft, abandoned launch vehicle stages, mission-related junk, and fragmentation debris.

Mercury 1

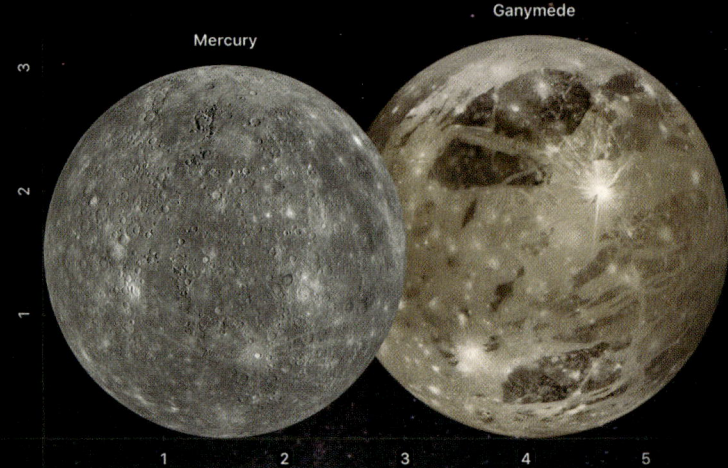

264 Mercury is the smallest of our solar system's planets. It has a diameter of 4,879 kilometres and is only marginally larger than our Moon. However, it is smaller than Jupiter's moon Ganymede and Saturn's moon Titan.

265 Mercury orbits the Sun more quickly than any other planet. For this reason, Mercury has been named after Mercurius, the Roman messenger of God who could travel very fast from one place to another.

266 Mercury's proximity to the Sun can make its surface temperature as high as 450°C, but at night the temperature can drop to -180°C, as the planet's thin atmosphere fails to trap heat.

267 Mercury's oval shaped orbit is highly elliptical; it takes the planet as close as 47 million kilometres and as far as 70 million kilometres from the Sun. Mercury completes one revolution around the Sun in 88 Earth days. Due to Mercury's slow rotation around its axis, a day on this planet is equal to 58 Earth days.

Mercury in "retrograde"

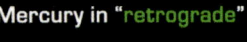 Sun
 Mercury
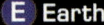 Earth

Path of Mercury in Earth's sky

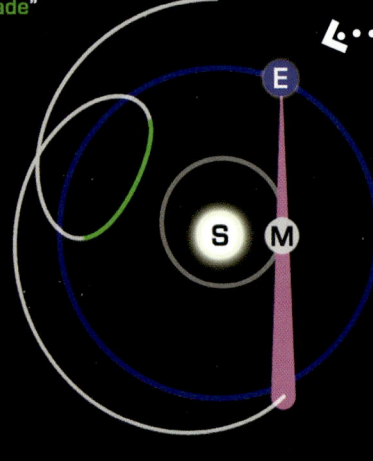

268 Since Mercury orbits the sun in 88 Earth days, while Earth takes 365, quite a few times a year, Mercury passes Earth on its journey around the sun, creating an optical illusion. Mercury appears to move "backwards" across the sky for around three weeks during this time and is said to be in retrograde.

269 Although Mercury is thought to have a solid inner core, its outer core is composed of a liquid metal. The iron core is about 2,100 km wide, making up nearly 85 percent of the planet's size. The crust and mantle combine to form a 400-kilometre-wide outer shell.

270 The rocky surface of Mercury is dark grey in colour and is covered with a thick layer of dust. The surface is believed to be made up of igneous silicate rocks and dust.

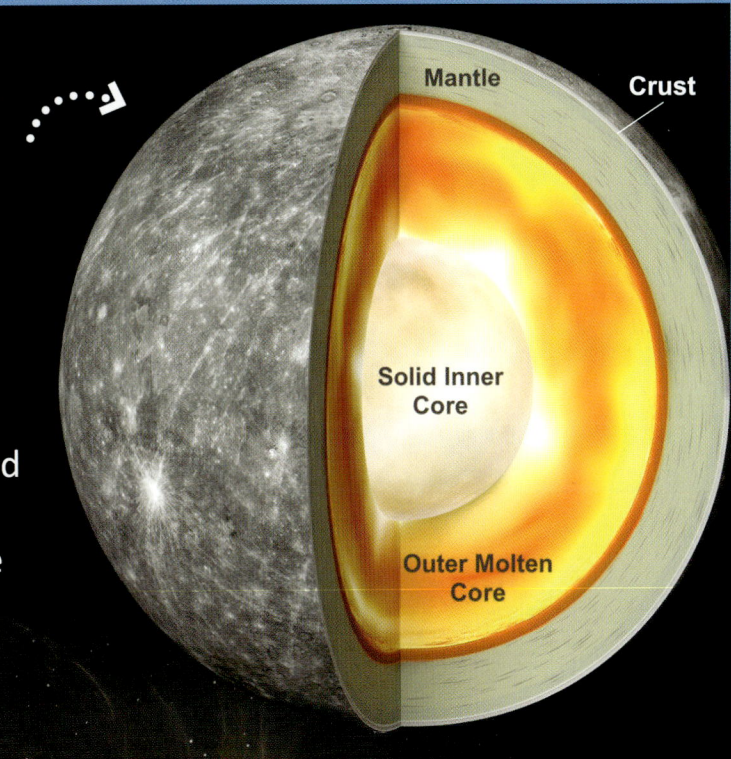

271 Mariner 10 was the first spacecraft to visit Mercury. It mapped about 45 percent of the planet's surface and detected its magnetic field. In 2011, MESSENGER visited Mercury and mapped the whole planet.

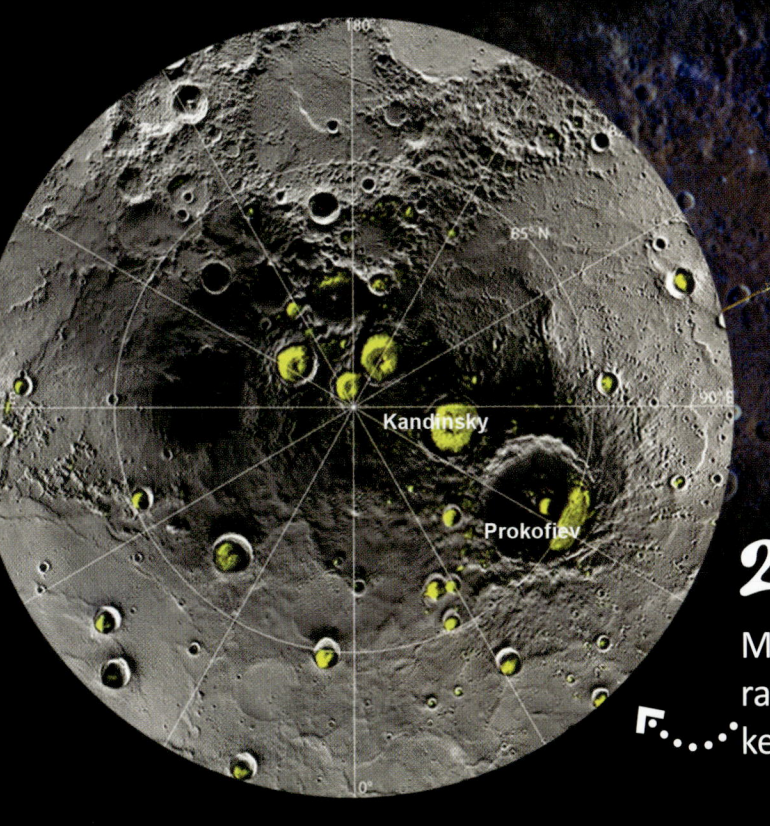

272 Water exists on Mercury in the form of water ice at the poles. Mercury's axis has no tilt, so its poles rarely receive any direct sunlight, which keeps the crater floors always in shadow.

Mercury 2

273 Mercury's surface is full of craters, but the "Caloris Basin" is the most stunning one. Craters larger than 300 kilometres are called *basins*. With a diameter of more than 1,500 kilometres, Caloris is one of the largest impact basins in the solar system. It is likely to have been created by a collision with a meteoroid or asteroid early in Mercury's history.

274 Mercury might have had an atmosphere when it was first formed, but frequent interactions with the solar wind have reduced it to a thin "surface bound exosphere". Additionally, due to its small size and weak gravity, the planet would not have been able to maintain the atmosphere.

275 Mercury has a thin, fuzzy tail, much like a comet. The sodium atoms in Mercury's atmosphere are ionised and dragged away by the Sun's radiation but are unable to escape Mercury's gravity, creating a bright "tail" glowing with orange-yellow light that extends from the planet's surface.

276 Studies show that in the 4.5 billion years since Mercury formed, its size has shrunk by many kilometres. This is happening because, unlike the other planets in the solar system, Mercury lacks an internal heat source. Mercury shrinks as its iron core cools and hardens, decreasing its overall volume.

277 NASA found a large geographical region called "Grand Valley" on Mercury. The structure is 1,000 kilometres long and 400 kilometres wide and is bigger than Arizona's Grand Canyon (on Earth). Grand Valley offers more proof of the planet's shrinkage.

278 Despite its slow spin, Mercury possesses a magnetic field. The strength of this magnetic field is around three times greater in the planet's northern hemisphere than in its southern one.

279 Due to its small size and closeness to the Sun, Mercury is the least-understood planet. Mercury can only be studied just before sunrise or shortly after sunset as its rising or setting is always within about two hours of the Sun's.

280 The cooling down of Mercury's core and its subsequent solidification causes wrinkles on its surface. Scientists have named these wrinkles "Lobate Scarps".

Missions to Mercury

281 A robotic space probe, Mariner 10, was launched by NASA on November 3, 1973, to study both Mercury and Venus in a single mission. It took 147 days to get from Earth to Mercury and made its first flyby on March 29, 1974, at a range of 703 kilometres.

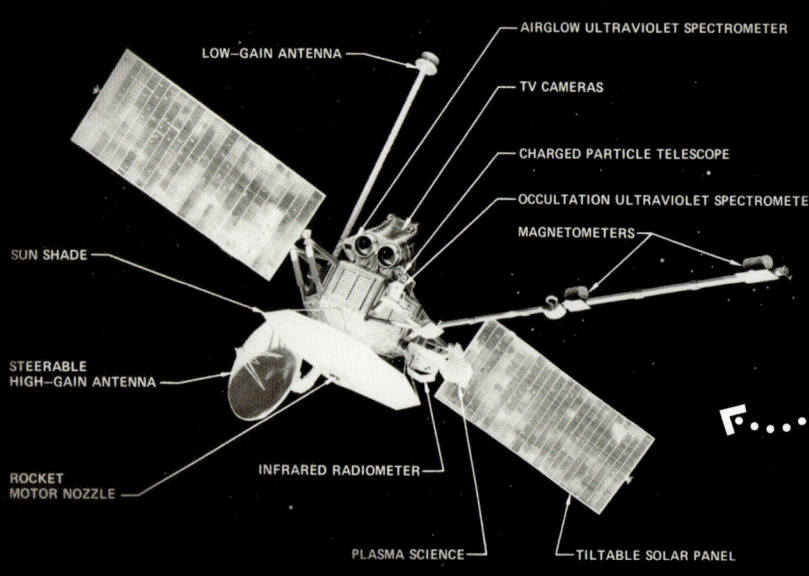

282 Mariner 10 was equipped with a variety of tools for researching the inner planets, including telescopes, cameras, magnetometers, infrared radiometers, and charged particle telescopes. It took more than 2,800 photos and mapped 40 to 45 percent of the planet's surface. It detected Mercury's weak atmosphere and the magnetic field as well as the ridges and the craters on its surface.

283 Mariner 10 was the first space probe to use the gravity of one planet (Venus) to reach another planet (Mercury). It also became the first spacecraft to control flight altitude using solar radiation pressure.

284 Mariner 10 flew by Mercury the second time on September 10, 1974, at a range of 48,069 kilometres. The third and the final flyby took place on March 16, 1975, at a very close range of only 327 kilometres.

285 MESSENGER (Mercury Surface Space Environment Geochemistry and Ranging), NASA's 7th spacecraft in Discovery mission, was launched on August 3, 2004 and, seven years later, on March 18, 2011, it finally entered Mercury's orbit. To reach Mercury it used several gravity-assist flybys through Earth and Venus and even Mercury.

286 The Mercury Atmosphere and Surface Composition Spectrometer (MASCS) was a unique device that was carried by the MESSENGER spacecraft. It made significant discoveries about Mercury's magnetic field, atmosphere, and surface. Additionally, it contributed to the creation of a vibrant spectral map of the planet with the help of the 200,000 photographs taken by it.

287 During its extended mission (March 18, 2012 to March 17, 2013) MESSENGER discovered frozen water in the craters at the poles, at places that never receive sunlight.

288 Launched on October 20, 2018, BepiColombo is a collaboration of European Space Agency (ESA) and Japanese Aerospace Exploration Agency (JAXA) to explore Mercury. It will reach Mercury on December 5, 2025, and is expected to start the operations by February 2026.

289 BepiColombo consists of two separate orbiters: the Mercury Magnetospheric Orbiter (MMO), to study the planet's magnetosphere, and the Mercury Planetary Orbiter (MPO), to map the planet.

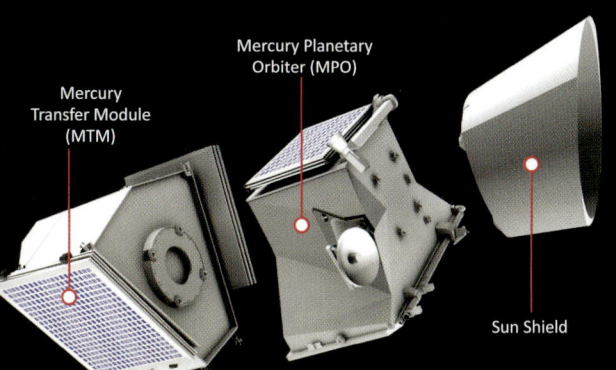

Mercury Transfer Module (MTM)
Mercury Planetary Orbiter (MPO)
Sun Shield
Mercury Magnetospheric Orbiter (MMO)

500 Fantastic Facts

Venus 1

290 Venus is the second terrestrial planet from the Sun and the hottest planet in the solar system. It is one of only two planets that rotate in the opposite way from the other planets.

291 On Venus, a day lasts longer than a year because of the very slow rotation of the planet on its axis. Venus rotates once around its axis in 243 Earth days (sidereal day) while it takes only 224 Earth days to complete one orbit around the Sun. On Venus, the Sun only rises every 117 Earth days (116 days 18 hrs), that is, twice a year, so the Venus solar day is 117 Earth days.

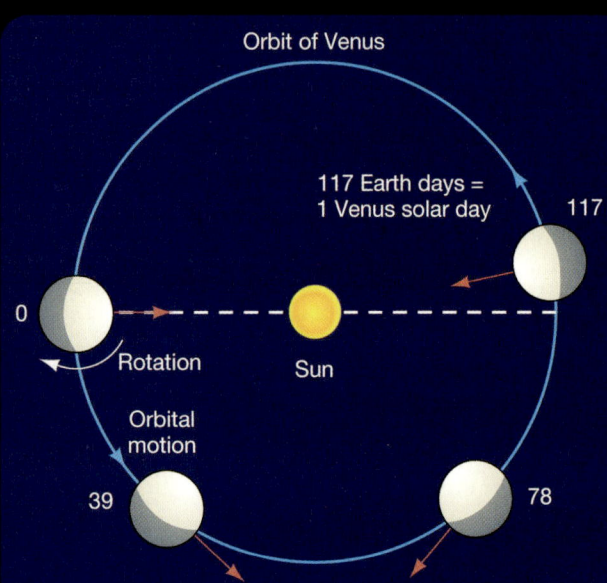

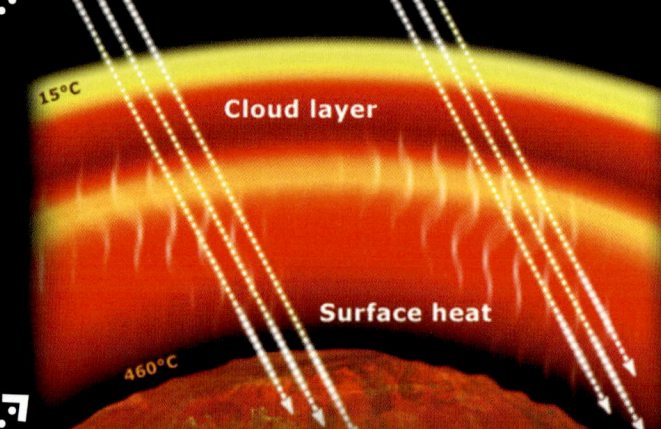

292 Despite being further from the Sun, Venus is hotter than Mercury. This is due to Venus's atmosphere having a high carbon dioxide concentration, which produces a strong greenhouse effect. It traps the heat like a blanket causing the surface temperature to reach 465°C.

293 After the Moon, Venus is the second-brightest natural object in the night sky. The clouds of sulphuric acid in Venus's atmosphere make it reflective and shiny, obscuring our view of its surface. Its brightness makes it visible at dusk and dawn, earning it the nickname of evening and morning star.

294 Venus was called by different names in different cultures. It was known as *Ishtar* by Babylonians, *Phosphoros* (morning star) and *Heosphoros* (evening star) by Greeks, *Chak ek* by Mayans, *Shukra* by Indians, and *Venus* by Romans.

295 Venus and Earth are sometimes called twins because of their similar size and mass. The mass of Venus is 4.868×10^{24} kg. That is about 82 percent of the mass of Earth. Venus has a diameter of 12,104 kilometres, only a few hundred kilometres less than that of Earth.

296 Carbon dioxide makes up the majority of Venus's atmosphere (96.5 percent), with a small percent of nitrogen (3.5 percent) and clouds of sulphuric acid. Carbon monoxide, argon, sulphur dioxide, and water vapour make up less than 1 percent. Compared to Earth, the atmosphere of Venus is denser and hotter.

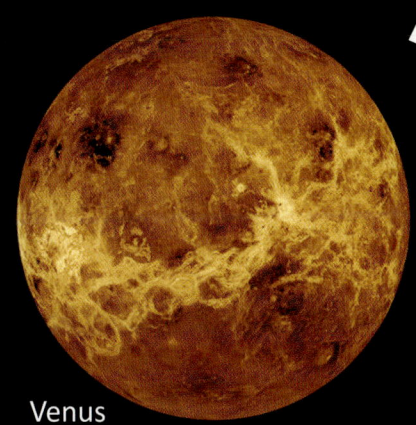

Venus   Earth

297 The atmospheric pressure on Venus is almost 90 times greater than on Earth! That is equivalent to the pressure in Earth's oceans at a depth of 1 kilometre.

Venus 2

298 According to recent scientific findings, Venus may have had surface water and been in a habitable state for around 3 billion years and may have remained in this state until 700–750 million years ago. A few million years ago, an unknown event caused a rise of carbon dioxide content in the Venusian atmosphere, transforming Venus into a hot, unfriendly planet.

299 Venus's interior is made up of a metallic iron core which is around 6,000 kilometres wide. The molten rocky mantle of Venus is around 3,000 kilometres thick. The thickness of the crust, which is mostly made up of basalt, is about 10 to 20 kilometres.

300 Venus does not have its own magnetic field. An induced magnetic field which is quite weak is created by the interaction of the Sun's magnetic field and the planet's outer atmosphere.

301 Venus has more volcanoes than any other planet in our solar system. High surface temperatures and the sulphuric acid clouds make it extremely difficult to study Venus. However, the images captured by space probes have confirmed the presence of fresh lava flows on the Venusian surface.

302 There are three terrae (major landmasses) on Venus that have been named. *Aphrodite Terra* is the largest one and is located just below the equator. *Lada Terra* is the second biggest in diameter, and it is in the southern polar region. *Ishtar Terra* is in the northern hemisphere.

303 On the surface of Venus, there are objects called coronae that are circular or oval shaped. They are thought to develop as a result of magma upwelling, which, when reaching the crust, melts, and collapses to produce these structures.

304 Like those on Earth, the mountain ranges on Venus are marked by numerous parallel folds and faults. The four main mountain ranges of Venus are named *Akna Montes, Danu Montes, Freyia Montes* and *Maxwell Montes*.

305 Venus transits happen when the planet is directly between the Sun and Earth at a certain point in its orbit. The event is rare and happens only four times every 243 years. The most recent two occurred in 2004 and 2012. The next transit will happen in 2117.

Missions to Venus

306 Between 1961 and 1984, the Soviet Union developed and launched a number of space probes under the Venera program. In Russian, the word Venera means "Venus." It created history by becoming the first program to launch human-built probes into another planet's atmosphere and to land safely there and use radar mapping to study a planet's surface.

307 Venera 13 (1981) continued to operate for two hours after touching down on the surface of Venus. It took both coloured and black-and-white pictures, drilled, and examined a sample of soil, and found that the soil was composed of volcanic ash.

308 On December 15, 1970, Venera 7 became the first human-made probe to transmit data from the surface of Venus. Though it made a bad landing due to parachute failure, it transmitted for 23 minutes after the impact. Despite the pressure sensor's failure, the temperature sensor showed that Venus' surface was a scorching 475°C.

309 Ten robotic interplanetary probes called Mariner were designed and developed by NASA's Jet Propulsion Laboratory (JPL) between 1962 and 1973, to explore the inner solar system planets: Venus, Mars, and Mercury. Among these probes, Mariner 1, 2, 5 and 10 were aimed at Venus.

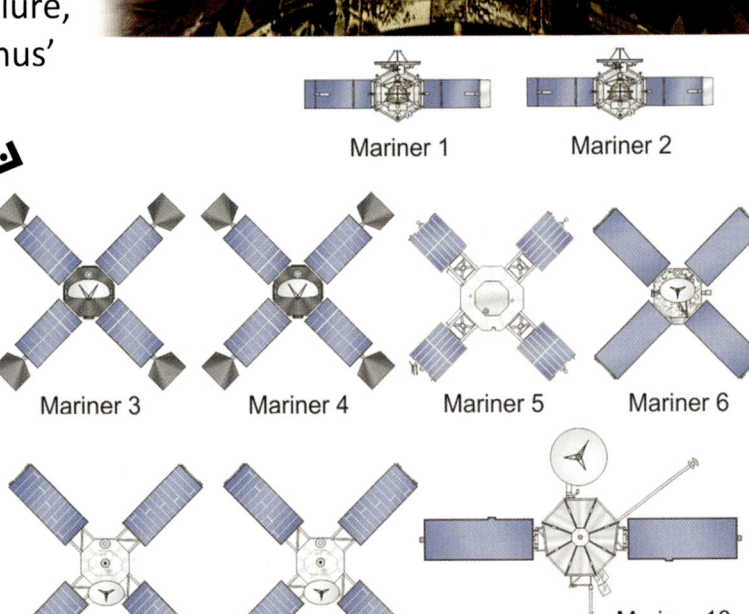

310 On July 22, 1962, Mariner 1 was launched, but it did not go off correctly. Mariner 2 was launched on August 27, 1962 and, after 110 days and travelling 34,773 kilometres, it successfully entered Venus's orbit.

311 NASA launched the Pioneer Venus mission in 1978 to explore the surface and atmosphere of Venus. It had two main components: Pioneer Venus Orbiter and Pioneer Venus Multiprobe, commonly known as Pioneer 12 and Pioneer 13 respectively.

312 On June 14, 1967, Mariner 5 was launched. The Venera 4 and Mariner 5 data were later studied together under a Soviet-American space cooperation group (COSPAR). The combined data revealed the presence of an extremely hot surface and a dense atmosphere on Venus.

313 Venus 1 (orbiter) discovered Venus to be smoother than Earth despite having a tall mountain (Maxwell Monte) and a deep canyon. The three identical probes of Pioneer 12 (Day, Night and North) analysed Venusian temperature and pressure.

314 The Mariner 10 was launched on November 3, 1973. It discovered evidence of rotating clouds and a very weak magnetic field. It captured images of Venus' chevron cloud using a near-ultraviolet filter.

500 Fantastic Facts

79

Earth 1

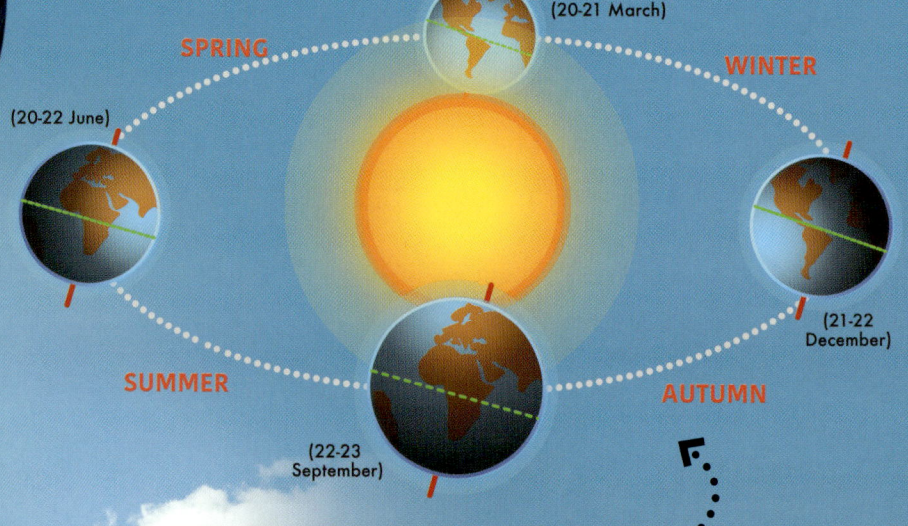

315 Earth is the third planet from the Sun and the fifth-largest planet in the solar system. It has an equatorial diameter of 12,756 kilometres and a polar diameter of 12,714 kilometres. Its ellipsoid shape makes it wider around the equator.

316 Earth's axis is tilted by 23.5 degrees from the plane of its orbit around the Sun. This tilt causes seasons. When the North Pole tilts toward the Sun, there is summer in the Northern Hemisphere. Similarly, the Southern Hemisphere experiences summer when the South Pole tilts toward the Sun.

317 Earth is unique as it is the only planet known to host life. It has tectonic plates and abundant water reservoirs that have played a crucial role in the evolution of complex life.

318 Earth was formed along with the other planets roughly 4.5 billion years ago from the material that was left over after the formation of the Sun. Young Earth was very hot with molten rocks due to frequent volcanic eruptions. It took Earth several billion years to cool down, and many millions more to become habitable.

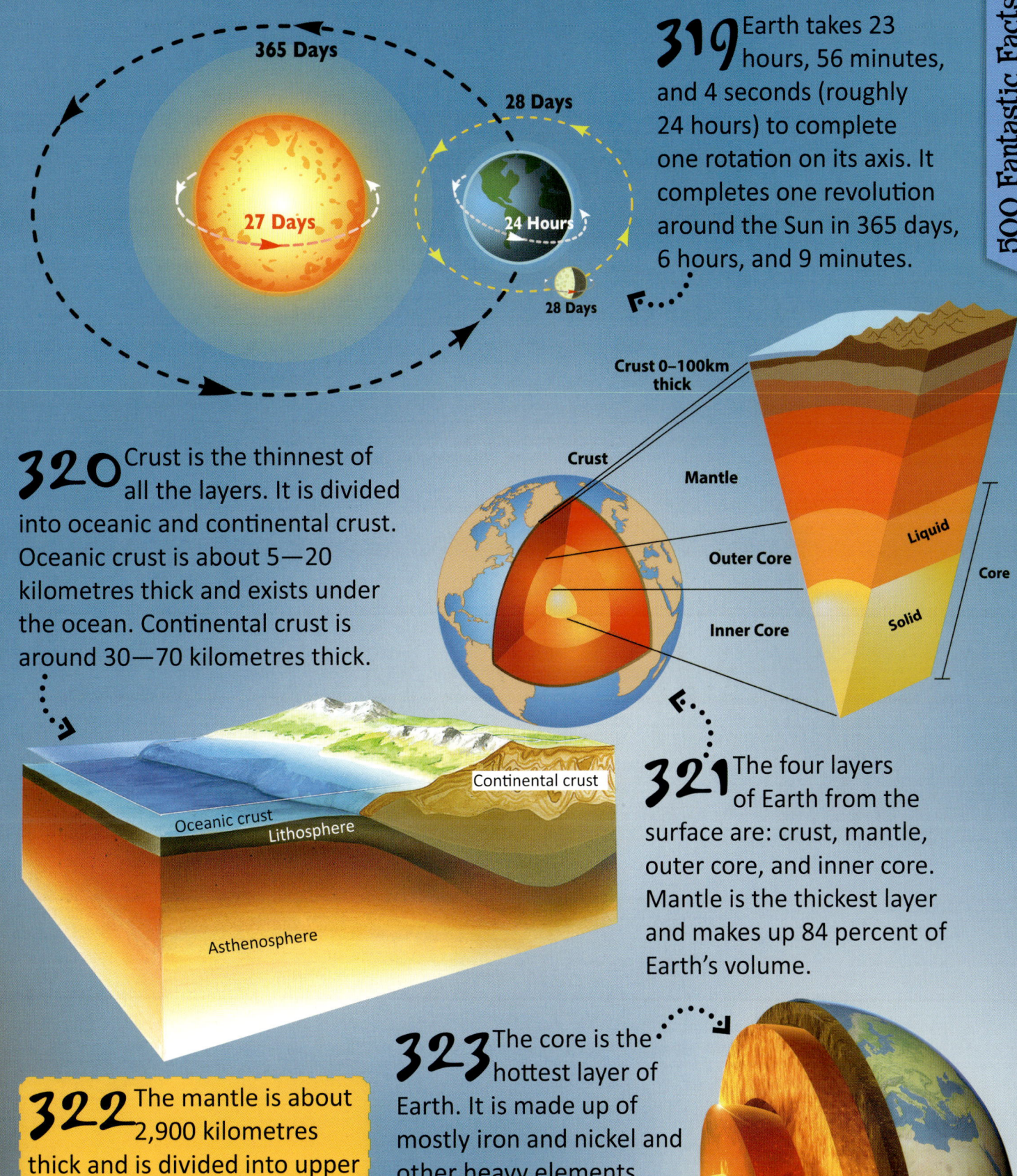

319 Earth takes 23 hours, 56 minutes, and 4 seconds (roughly 24 hours) to complete one rotation on its axis. It completes one revolution around the Sun in 365 days, 6 hours, and 9 minutes.

320 Crust is the thinnest of all the layers. It is divided into oceanic and continental crust. Oceanic crust is about 5—20 kilometres thick and exists under the ocean. Continental crust is around 30—70 kilometres thick.

321 The four layers of Earth from the surface are: crust, mantle, outer core, and inner core. Mantle is the thickest layer and makes up 84 percent of Earth's volume.

322 The mantle is about 2,900 kilometres thick and is divided into upper and lower mantle. Crust and the upper mantle form the lithosphere. The distribution of heat and material in the mantle influences Earth's topography.

323 The core is the hottest layer of Earth. It is made up of mostly iron and nickel and other heavy elements. The metal in the outer core is in liquid form. Its constant churning creates the planet's magnetic field. The inner core is a solid ball of iron.

500 Fantastic Facts

Earth 2

324 Asteroid and meteorite impacts, along with volcanic activity, were frequent in Earth's early history. Life forms may have evolved with the aid of the heat, chemical elements, and water provided by asteroids and lava, as well as the organic molecules.

325 For many years there has been a long debate on the age of the oldest fossils found. With the help of research, led by palaeobiologist William Schopf and geoscientist John Valley, we now know that bacteria and microbes existed nearly 3.5 billion years ago.

326 Living organisms that evolved early in Earth's history are called primitive life forms. They were simple life forms that could survive in harsh conditions such as viruses and cyanobacteria.

327 The early atmosphere consisted of methane, steam, and carbon dioxide. As oceans formed, carbon dioxide started dissolving in water. A basic type of bacteria eventually emerged, consuming the water's carbon dioxide and sunlight while exuding oxygen as a byproduct.

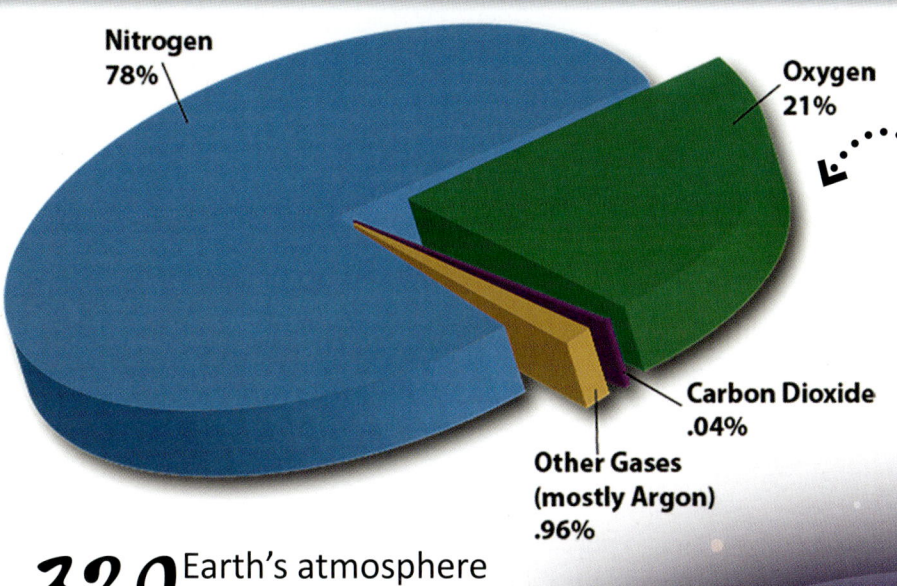

328 The thin layer of gases surrounding Earth form a protective blanket known as the atmosphere. It is made up of nitrogen (78 percent), oxygen (20.9 percent), argon (0.9 percent) and trace quantities of carbon dioxide, water vapour and other gases.

329 Earth's atmosphere consists of five main layers. From lowest to highest, they are: troposphere, stratosphere, mesosphere, thermosphere, and exosphere. Troposphere is the layer closest to Earth. Commercial passenger planes fly in the lower stratosphere. Mesosphere is the layer where most meteors burn up. Exosphere is the uppermost layer; it separates the rest of the atmosphere from outer space.

330 The ozone is the protective shield in the stratosphere, 15—35 kilometres above Earth's surface. It protects us from Sun's harmful ultraviolet (UV) radiations. The UV light causes sunburn, skin infections, skin cancer (melanoma) and premature ageing. The ozone layer absorbs about 98 percent of this harmful UV radiation.

UV protection by the ozone layer

Moon 1

331 The Moon is the only natural satellite of Earth. It is one fourth the size of our planet and measures 3,476 in diameter. It is the fifth largest moon in the solar system and the largest satellite relative to the size of the planet it revolves around.

332 The Moon is thought to have formed some 4.5 billion years ago when a Mars sized planet collided with proto-Earth. The impact sent material into orbit around Earth, where it accumulated and eventually became the Moon.

333 Moon's phases could be easily observed without the use of complex instruments. For this reason, astronomical calendars were in use during ancient times where the month lasted 28 days. Even in recent times, in many cultures, the first day of a month begins on a new moon.

334 The average distance between Moon and Earth is 384,400 kilometres. Due to its elliptical orbit of revolution the distance of the Moon from Earth is not the same everywhere along its orbit. It is 405,696 kilometres at its farthest and 363,105 kilometres at its nearest.

335 In the absence of a strong atmosphere, the Moon was continuously bombarded by asteroids and comets: leaving the surface with large impact craters. A charcoal grey powdery dust called lunar regolith covers the entire surface. The fractured bedrock below it is called the megaregolith. The dark areas of the Moon are called maria and the light regions are known as highlands.

336 In 2008, the Indian spacecraft Chandrayan-1 was the first mission to confirm the presence of surface water ice on Moon using the onboard "Moon Mineralogy Mapper". Later, other missions such as Lunar Prospector, LCROSS, and Lunar Reconnaissance Orbiter have shown the presence of high concentrations of ice water in the shadowed regions of the lunar poles.

337 We always see the same side of the Moon because it is tidally locked to Earth: that is, it rotates on its axis at the same time as it revolves around Earth.

The moon rotates one time for every revolution around the earth

338 The exosphere, the Moon's thin and weak atmosphere, provides no defence against solar radiation or strikes from comets and meteoroids. A permanent dust cloud exists around the Moon, produced by small particles from comets.

Moon 2

339 When we view from Earth, the air filters the reflected light making the Moon appear red or blue depending on its angle in the sky, the thickness of the atmosphere and the particles in the air.

Blue Moon   Red Moon

340 Since prehistoric times people have taken note of the Moon's phases and have used Tally Sticks to keep records. The discovery of a 20,000-year-old notched animal bone is proof of this fact.

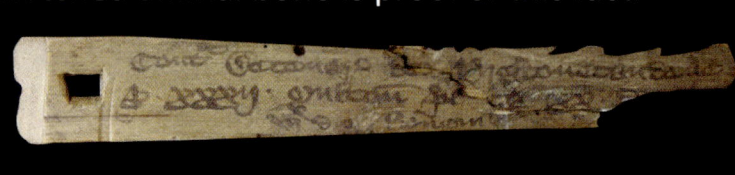

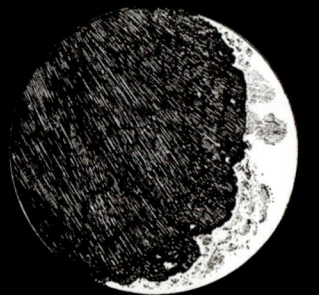

341 In 1609, Galileo Galilei became the first man to watch the Moon from a telescope. He observed the surface of the Moon and found that it was full of mountains and craters. *Sidereus Nuncius*, Galileo's Moon sketches, was the first ever publication that gave a description of the Moon's topography.

342 The Luna program of the Soviet Union was the first to achieve a number of objectives. In 1959, Luna 1 was the first spacecraft to reach near Moon, Luna 2 was the first to land on its surface and Luna 3 was the first to take pictures of its far side. Rock and soil samples were brought back by Luna 16, 20 and 24 ((1970—1976).

343 Unlike the Soviet's robotic missions, the United States planned a manned Moon landing. In preparation for human missions, the US launched various uncrewed probes. "Ranger program" provided lunar close-up images, "Orbiter program" produced maps of the entire Moon, and the "Surveyor program" demonstrated soft landing on the Moon.

344 In 1968, Apollo-8 became the first crewed spacecraft to reach the Moon and orbit around it ten times without landing. Astronauts Frank Borman, James A. Lovell and William A. Anders were the first humans to see the far side of the Moon.

345 In January 2019, Chang E-4, launched by China's CNSA made history by becoming the first spacecraft to touch down successfully on the South Pole-Aitken basin, on the far side of the Moon.

346 Numerous nations, (including the USA, the Soviet Union, Japan, India China and Isarel) and the ESA, have launched probes to the Moon. However, only three countries (the Soviet Union, the United States, and China) have successfully landed a spacecraft on the lunar surface.

347 To further explore the Moon, NASA is now developing the "Artemis program", which aims to make its first lunar south pole touchdown by 2025. The Artemis program is carried out by NASA in collaboration with US commercial spaceflight contractors, and the European Space Agency. Through the signing of the Artemis Accords, other nations have been invited to join the initiative. This accord has already been signed by 21 countries.

Moon Landing

348 NASA's "Apollo 11", carrying Neil Armstrong, Buzz Aldrin, and Michael Collins, headed for the Moon on July 16, 1969. It entered Moon's orbit on July 19. On July 20, Armstrong and Aldrin landed on the Moon in the lunar module Eagle while Collins stayed in the command module Columbia, orbiting the Moon.

349 The lunar module Eagle landed on the Moon in the *Sea of Tranquillity* at 20.17 UTC on July 20, 1969. As soon as the module touched the lunar surface, Armstrong radioed his famous message to mission control: "Eagle has landed".

350 On July 21 at 2.56 UTC, six hours after the Eagle landing, Armstrong became the first man to step foot on the Moon and declared proudly: "That is one small step for a man, one giant leap for mankind." He was joined by Buzz Aldrin 19 minutes later and together they planted the US flag.

351 They collected soil and rock samples and performed a few simple experiments. Aldrin's simple words describing Moon were: "magnificent desolation". Armstrong mounted the TV camera and the world saw another land for the first time.

352 Apart from the flag, a plaque that read: "Here men from the planet Earth first set foot on the Moon - July 1969 A.D. We came in peace for all mankind." was left behind on the Moon.

353 Armstrong and Aldrin stayed on the Moon's surface for a total of 21 and a half hours. After collecting 21.5 kilograms of lunar rocks as samples they left the lunar surface to meet up with Michael Collins in the command module that was orbiting above. On July 24, 1969, they finally made it safely back to Earth and landed in the Pacific Ocean.

354 Michael Collins captured this image of the eagle with Armstrong and Aldrin inside and with Earth in the background, as the lunar module rose from the Moon's surface to connect with the command module.

Pete Conrad

355 In all, 24 American astronauts made the trip from Earth to the Moon between 1968 and 1972 and 12 of them walked on the lunar surface. They include Charles "Pete" Conrad, the third person to set foot on the Moon. Some of the later astronauts were Alan Bean, Alan B. Shephard, Edgar D. Mitchell, David R. Scott, and James B. Irwin.

Mars 1

356 Mars looks red because of the presence of lots of iron oxide in its surface material. At the time of formation, due to Mars's smaller size and weaker gravity, much of the iron stayed on its upper layers. The continuous oxidisation of this iron makes the surface of Mars looks red or rust coloured.

357 Mars is named after the Roman God of War. Since the red colour is associated with blood, in most of the civilisations Mars is named after their God of war. Greeks called it "Ares", Egyptians named it "Her Desher", and the Chinese called it the "fire star".

Earth

Mars

358 Mars is the fourth planet from the Sun. It is about half the size of Earth. It has a diameter of 6,791 kilometres which is a little more than Earth's radius.

359 The distance between Mars and the Sun is 228 million kilometres. Mars takes 687 Earth days to make one complete trip around the Sun. One day on Mars is 24 hours and 36 minutes.

Mars Orbit
Earth Orbit

1 Earth Year = 365 days
1 Mars Year = 687 Earth days or 669 sols (martian days)

360 Mars has canyons, volcanoes, dried lake beds, and craters all over its rocky surface. Like Earth, Mars has wind and clouds. It frequently experiences huge red dust storms. Small dust storms look like tornadoes and the large ones can be seen by telescopes on Earth.

361 Due to its greater distance from the Sun, the average temperature on Mars is -60°C. It can vary from -125°C near the poles during winter to 20°C near the equator at midday.

362 The atmosphere of Mars consists of 95.32 percent carbon dioxide, 2.7 percent nitrogen, 1.6 percent argon, 0.13 percent oxygen and trace amounts of water vapour and other gases.

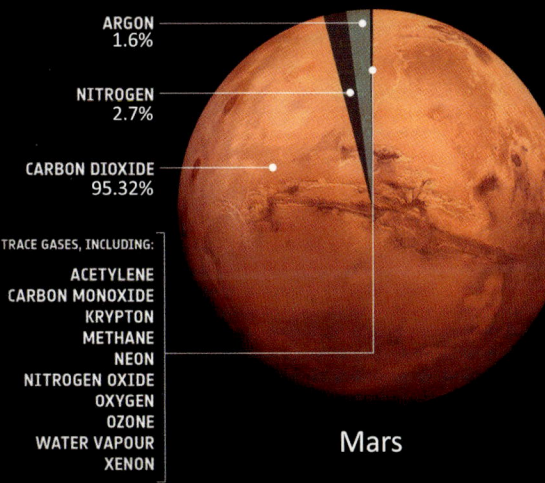

Mars
- ARGON 1.6%
- NITROGEN 2.7%
- CARBON DIOXIDE 95.32%
- TRACE GASES, INCLUDING: ACETYLENE, CARBON MONOXIDE, KRYPTON, METHANE, NEON, NITROGEN OXIDE, OXYGEN, OZONE, WATER VAPOUR, XENON

Earth
- OXYGEN 20.9%
- NITROGEN 78.1%
- TRACE GASES, INCLUDING: ARGON (0.93%), CARBON DIOXIDE, HELIUM, HYDROGEN, KRYPTON, METHANE, NEON, NITROUS OXIDE, OZONE, SULPHUR DIOXIDE, WATER VAPOUR, XENON

363 At the north and south poles, layered stacks of water ice and dust, called polar ice caps, are found. The top unit, "seasonal ice cap", forms during Martian winter and fall. The "residual ice cap", which has been there for centuries, is underneath it. The "polar layered deposit" is hundreds of thousands of years old. The polar ice caps' "basal units" date back at least billions of years.

Mars 2

364 The thin atmosphere of Mars is unable to shield the planet's surface from sun rays. Since it contains so little oxygen, it is not suited for living things. According to studies, Mars used to have a thicker atmosphere and may have had oceans and even freshwater lakes and rivers billions of years ago.

365 Around 4 billion years ago, Mars lost its magnetic field which allowed the solar wind to largely strip the planet of its atmosphere. The shutting down of iron-core dynamo billions of years ago is the reason behind the loss of the magnetic field.

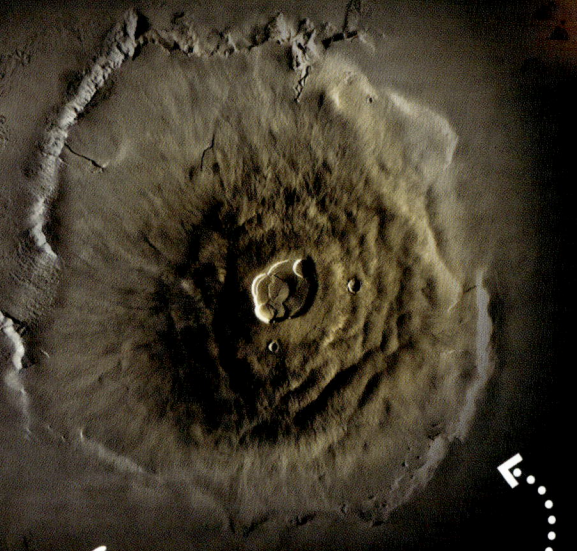

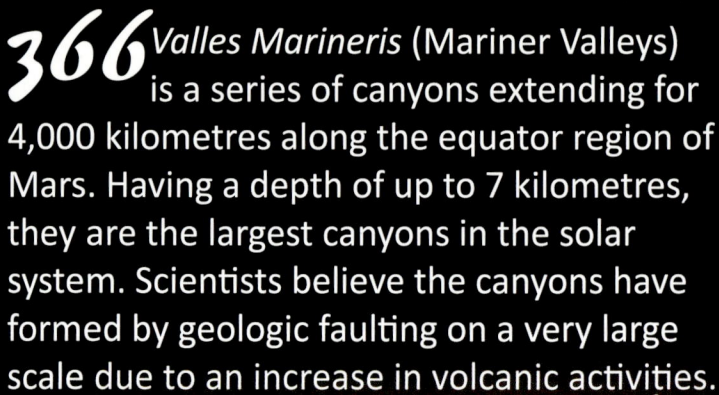

366 *Valles Marineris* (Mariner Valleys) is a series of canyons extending for 4,000 kilometres along the equator region of Mars. Having a depth of up to 7 kilometres, they are the largest canyons in the solar system. Scientists believe the canyons have formed by geologic faulting on a very large scale due to an increase in volcanic activities.

367 *Olympus Mons* is the largest volcano in the entire solar system. Found on Mars it is a large shield volcano having a diameter of 600 kilometres and a height of 21 kilometres, over twice the height of Earth's Mt. Everest.

368 The core of Mars mainly consists of iron and nickel and a small amount of sulphur. It is surrounded by a silicate mantle. The crust is mostly made up of volcanic rock basalt.

369 Gravity is very weak on Mars because of its smaller mass. Mars has 38 percent less gravity than Earth has. Thus, compared to Earth, you could jump three times higher on Mars.

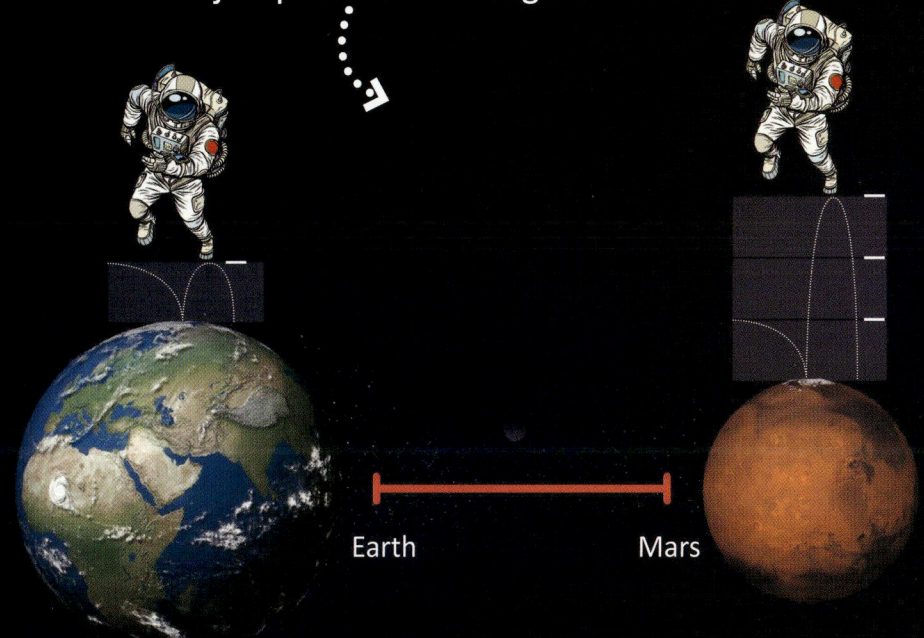

370 Data collected from spacecraft shows that Mars has four possible reservoirs of water: in its atmosphere containing water vapour, in the frozen water at its polar caps, in its sub-surface, and in the water which is chemically locked up in rocks and minerals.

371 Mars has an axial tilt of 25°, which means, just like Earth, Mars has four seasons, but they last twice as long. This happens because Mars takes about two Earth years to complete an orbit around the Sun.

Mars's Moons

372 Phobos and Deimos are the two moons of Mars. They are the smallest moons in the solar system. Phobos is larger than Deimos and orbits Mars at 6,000 kilometres. It travels around Mars thrice a day while Deimos takes 30 hours to complete a revolution. Phobos is 22 kilometers long while Deimos is only 13 kilometers. Both moons orbit the red planet in stable, nearly circular orbits.

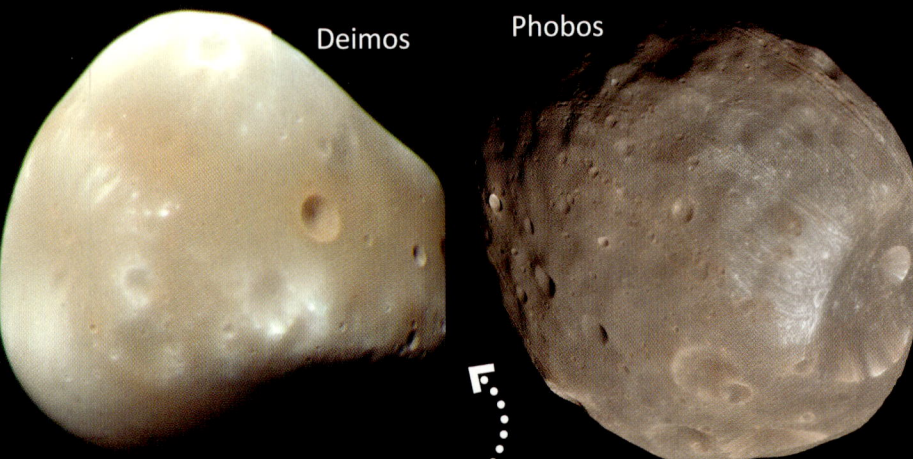

373 Both Phobos and Deimos were discovered by the American astronomer Asaph Hall III in the year 1877. He named the moons for the mythological sons of Ares. Phobos means fear and Deimos means dread.

374 Due to their small size and insufficient mass, the gravity of Phobos and Deimos cannot pull them into the shape of spheres like planets or other moons. For this reason, both the moons are irregular in shape.

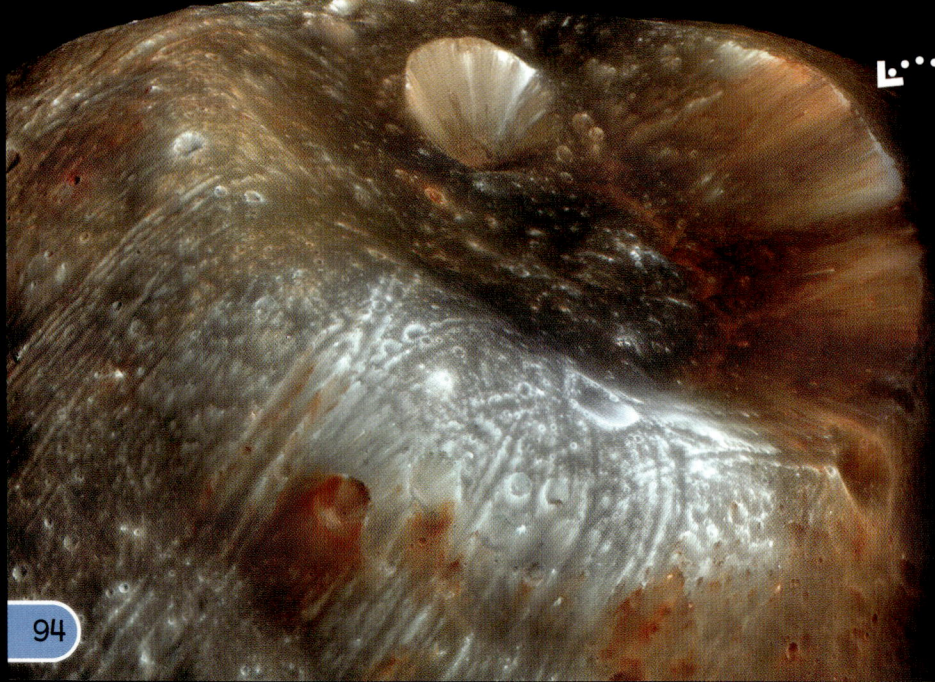

375 The craters on each of Mars's moons are the result of meteor strikes. Stickney crater on Phobos is a 9-kilometre-wide pit. It is almost half the diameter of Phobos. There is an intricate network of grooves around this crater which probably formed due to the impact.

376 The origin of Mars's moons is the subject of numerous theories. One theory holds that the two moons are asteroids captured from the asteroid belt. But they orbit Mars in a regular, spherical manner. This suggests that the moons were created either by collision or formed during the formation of the planet itself.

Deimos

Phobos

craters

377 Phobos is moving inwards towards Mars at a rate of 1.8 metres every century. In 50 million years, Phobos is predicted to either collide with Mars or break up into small bits and form a ring of fragments around the planet. Deimos, on the other hand, is steadily moving away from Mars.

378 Both Phobos and Deimos have a surface covered in numerous craters and are dark grey in colour. They are composed of the same substances that are similar to carbonaceous chondrites, the component found in asteroids.

379 NASA's Mariner 9 was the first spacecraft to take pictures of Phobos and Deimos while orbiting Mars in 1971. Some great images and videos of the moons were captured by the Curiosity rover. One piece of footage shows Phobos eclipsing the Sun away from Mars.

Missions to Mars

380 NASA's Mariner 4 spacecraft, which was launched in 1964, was the first to safely fly by Mars and obtain a close-up picture of the red planet. It took 4 days for the data to reach Earth after it was transmitted.

381 The 1969 launch of the identical Mariner 6 and Mariner 7 spacecraft brought them within 3,430 kilometres of Mars. The spacecraft revealed details on the size, mass, and shape of the planet as well as the existence of carbon dioxide-based ice caps on Mars's south pole.

382 Launched in May 1971, Mariner 9 reached Mars in November of the same year. It was the first spacecraft to orbit another planet. Upon arrival, it faced a severe Martian dust storm and had to wait a couple of months. After spending 349 days in Mars's orbit, it imaged 85 percent of the surface and shared images of riverbeds, craters, Olympus Mons, canyons and the two moons.

383 The Viking project was the first successful US mission to land a spacecraft on the Martian surface. Viking 1 and 2 were identical spacecraft, each having a lander and an orbiter. In addition to capturing pictures and gathering scientific data, three biology experiments were carried out by the two landers to check for potential signs of life.

384 A Mars rover is a robotic vehicle that is specifically designed to travel on the surface of Mars. As of May 2021, there have been five rovers by the NASA's Jet Propulsion Laboratory: Sojourner, Opportunity, Spirit, Curiosity and Perseverance. The sixth rover is Zhurong, which is managed by the China National Space Administration.

385 Spirit and Opportunity, the twin rovers, were sent to Mars in 2004 to find out signs of past water on Mars. They were landed on opposite sides of the planet. The photos taken by the rovers and the rocks studied by them showed that there were once lakes and rivers on the Martian surface.

386 Curiosity is a car-sized robot that was originally planned for two years, but in 2012 its mission was extended indefinitely. It completed ten years on August 6, 2022. Its mission goals were to explore Mars's climate, geology, and planetary habitability.

387 Perseverance was launched in 2020 (landed in 2021) to investigate the *Jezero Crater* on Mars. Its design is similar to Curiosity, albeit slightly upgraded. It carries a mini-helicopter *Ingenuity* to assist in scouting the area for intriguing spots to explore.

388 Scientists are considering Mars colonisation in the years to come but it is a challenging process. Humans could only survive on Mars in artificial habitats that simulate conditions on Earth. Terraforming and establishing a Mars base camp are the proposed missions. Terraforming is a process in which a hostile land is transformed into a fertile one.

Jupiter 1

389 The light and dark bands seen on Jupiter's surface are made of cold and windy clouds containing crystals of frozen ammonia, water vapour, water ice and some other chemicals. The dark bands are called belts and the light ones are called zones. Zones are colder than belts.

390 Jupiter is the largest planet in the solar system. The planet is twice as massive as all the other planets combined. It is named after Jupiter, the king of gods in ancient Rome, because of its enormous size.

391 According to the current model of our solar system, Jupiter was likely the first planet to have formed. Primarily, made up of gases left over from the formation of the Sun, Jupiter could have become a star if it had been 80 times more massive.

392 Jupiter has rings too, but they are not as noticeable as Saturn's. The three faint rings of Jupiter are made of dust particles.

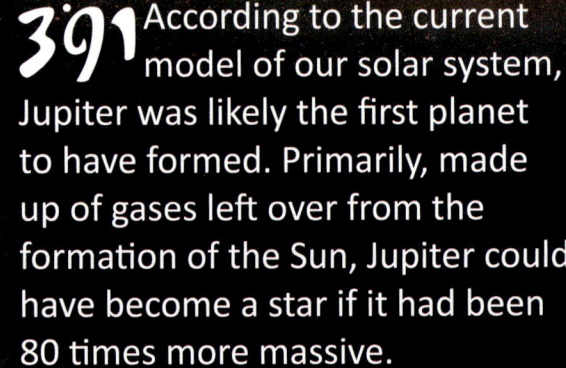

393 The Great Red Spot is a giant, spinning storm on Jupiter that has lasted more than 300 years. The spot is twice the size of Earth. Observations show that the size of the storm is decreasing by about 930 kilometres every year.

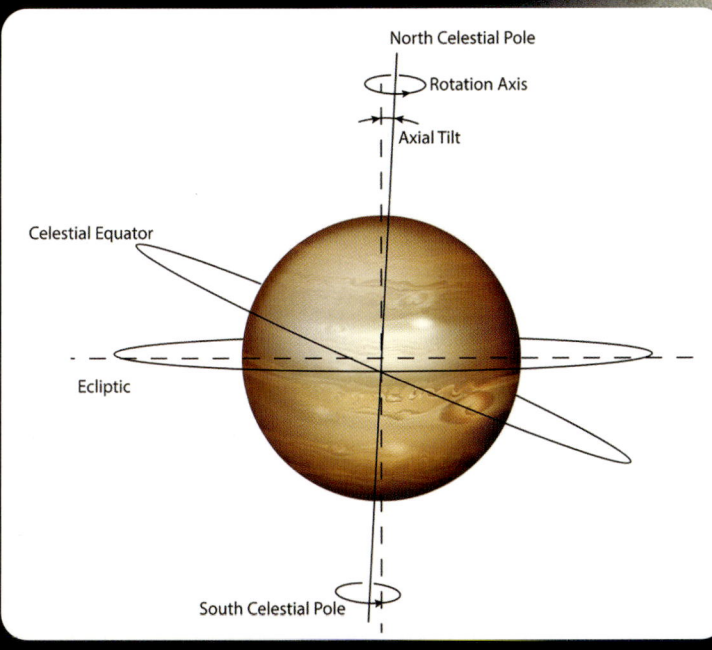

394 The average distance between Jupiter and the Sun is 778 million kilometres. It takes about 11.86 Earth years to complete one orbit around the Sun.

395 Jupiter has the shortest day of all the planets in our solar system because it rotates very fast on its axis. A day on Jupiter is only 10 hours long. Only a 3 degree tilt is present between its equator and its orbital path around the Sun. This means Jupiter rotates nearly upright and does not have extreme seasons like other planets.

396 Jupiter has the largest atmosphere in the solar system. Just like the Sun, the atmosphere is mostly composed of molecular hydrogen and helium. Other chemical elements (such as methane, ammonia, hydrogen sulphide, and water) are only found in trace amounts.

Jupiter 2

397 Jupiter has the strongest magnetic field of all planets in the solar system. The magnetic field is probably generated by a swirling mass of hydrogen deep within the planet. Jupiter's moon Io also provides a significant amount of charged particles to the magnetosphere.

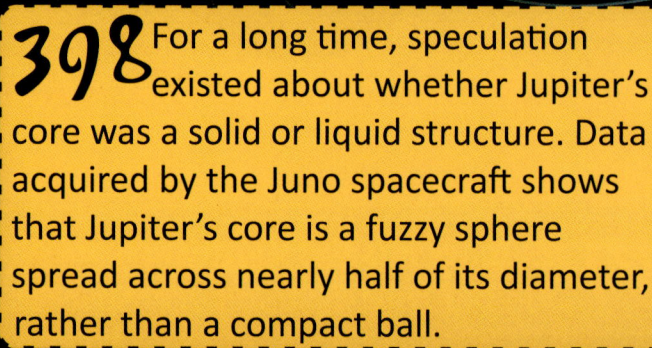

398 For a long time, speculation existed about whether Jupiter's core was a solid or liquid structure. Data acquired by the Juno spacecraft shows that Jupiter's core is a fuzzy sphere spread across nearly half of its diameter, rather than a compact ball.

399 Jupiter has the brightest and most intense auroras in the solar system. These auroras are caused by solar storms and charged particles tossed by its moon Io.

400 As a gas giant, Jupiter lacks a true surface and is instead made up of many layers of hydrogen and helium gas clouds that convert into liquid hydrogen, as we go down, due to high pressure. Deep down the liquid is electrically charged. The core might be solid or liquid.

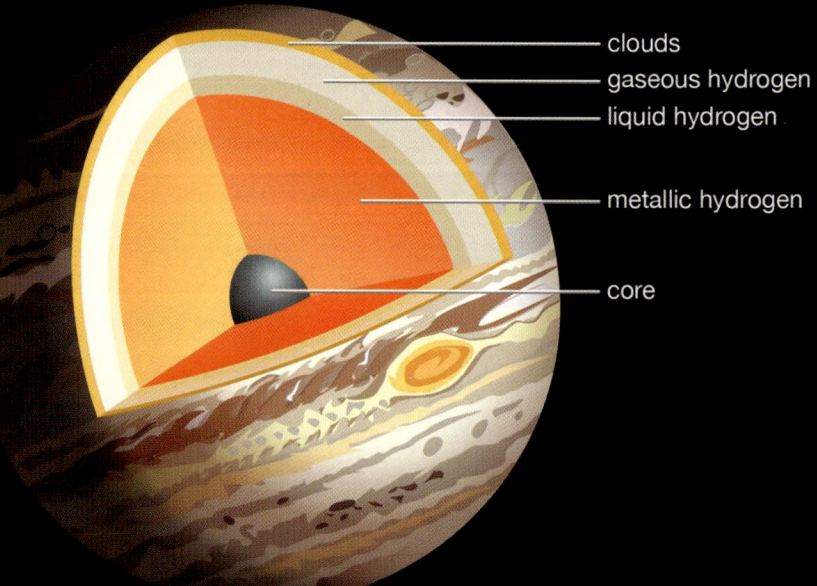

clouds
gaseous hydrogen
liquid hydrogen
metallic hydrogen
core

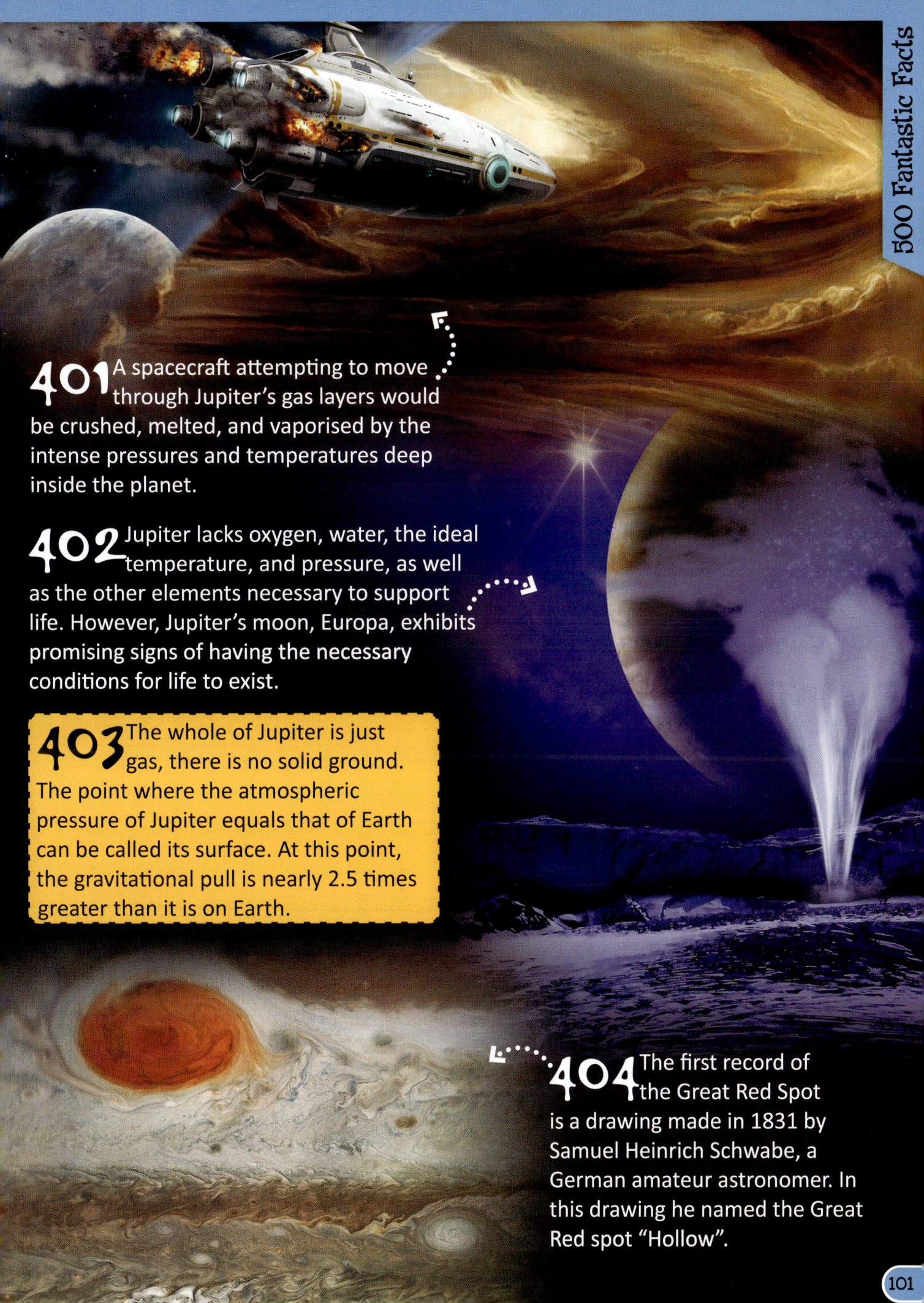

500 Fantastic Facts

401 A spacecraft attempting to move through Jupiter's gas layers would be crushed, melted, and vaporised by the intense pressures and temperatures deep inside the planet.

402 Jupiter lacks oxygen, water, the ideal temperature, and pressure, as well as the other elements necessary to support life. However, Jupiter's moon, Europa, exhibits promising signs of having the necessary conditions for life to exist.

403 The whole of Jupiter is just gas, there is no solid ground. The point where the atmospheric pressure of Jupiter equals that of Earth can be called its surface. At this point, the gravitational pull is nearly 2.5 times greater than it is on Earth.

404 The first record of the Great Red Spot is a drawing made in 1831 by Samuel Heinrich Schwabe, a German amateur astronomer. In this drawing he named the Great Red spot "Hollow".

101

Jupiter's Moons

Io

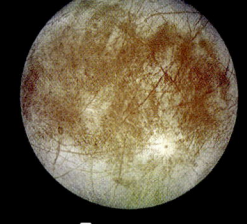
Europa

Ganymede

Callisto

405 Jupiter has 79 moons in total, 53 of which are given names. Europa, Io, Ganymede, and Callisto are the four biggest moons. They were discovered by Galileo and are thus known as Galilean satellites in honour of him.

406 Ganymede is the biggest moon in the solar system. With a diameter of 5,268 kilometres, it is even bigger than the planet Mercury. Ganymede is the only moon to have an internally generated magnetic field.

407 Based on the observation by NASA's Galileo mission that flew by Ganymede in 1990, scientists suggest that the moon might have a pile of ocean layers separated by different phases of ice.

408 Io is the most volcanically active celestial body in the solar system. Its high volcanic activity is the result of a tussle between Jupiter's strong gravity and the pulls by two nearby moons: Europa and Ganymede.

409 More than 150 volcanoes may be found on the surface of Io, some of which can erupt sulphur plumes up to 300 kilometres in the air. Numerous lava lakes and floodplains with molten rocks are also present on the surface.

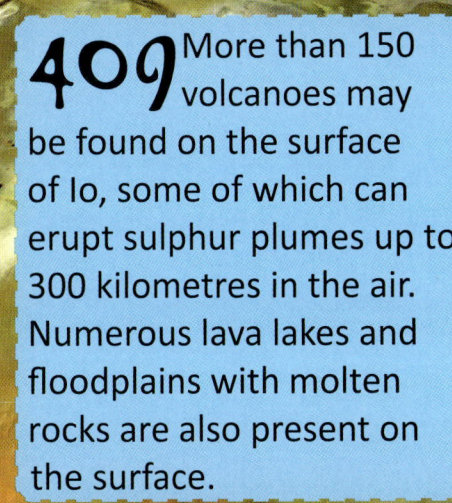

410 The surface of Europa is almost entirely covered in ice. Scientists predict the presence of a liquid ocean beneath the ice. Its smooth and icy surface makes Europa the brightest moon in the solar system.

411 Europa has a diameter that is only one-fourth that of Earth, but it is thought to have twice as much water. Scientists consider this moon to be a potential habitable zone because of its immensely deep ocean.

412 Callisto is Jupiter's second largest moon and the oldest moon in the solar system. With a surface full of craters, it is also the most heavily cratered body in our solar system.

Saturn 1

413 Saturn is the second largest planet in our solar system. It is a gas giant, made mostly out of hydrogen and helium. The planet is named after Jupiter's father, who was the Roman God of agriculture and wealth.

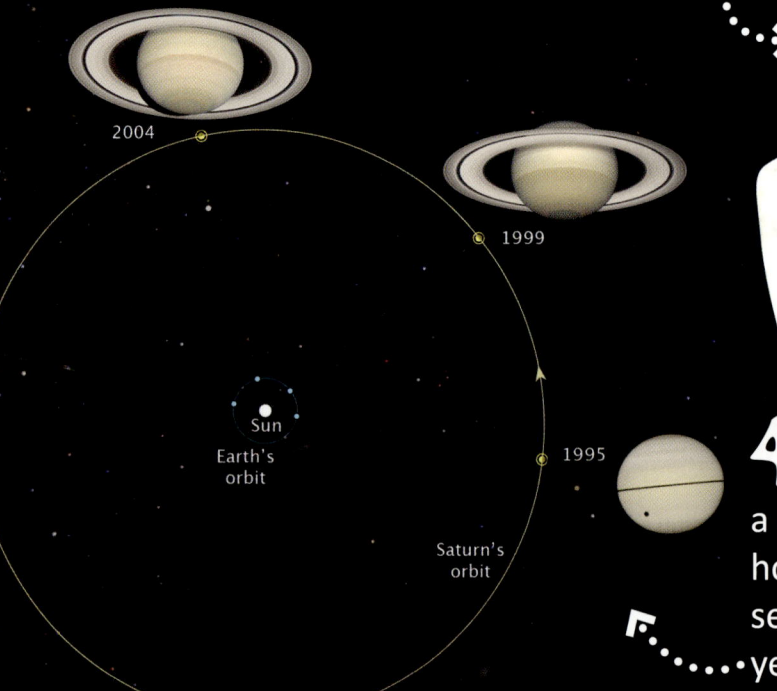

414 Saturn has a very fast rotational speed; a day on Saturn is only 10 hours, 33 minutes, and 38 seconds. It takes 29.4 Earth years to complete one orbit around the Sun.

415 Saturn is among the five planets that are visible from Earth without a telescope. Though distant, it has been observed and recorded by many ancient cultures. Saturday, the day of the week, got its name from the Roman God, Saturn.

416 Saturn contains 96.3 percent hydrogen and 3.25 percent helium in its outer atmosphere. The upper clouds are made up of ammonia crystals, while the lower-level clouds consist of either ammonium hydrosulphide or water.

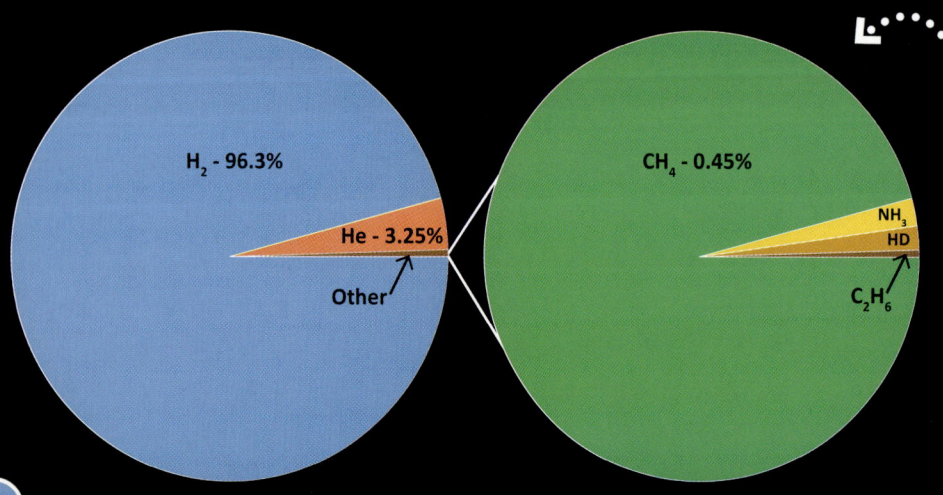

417 A core of iron-nickel and rock presumably makes up Saturn's interior. A deep layer of metallic hydrogen surrounds its core, followed by an intermediate layer of liquid hydrogen and liquid helium, and lastly there is a gaseous outer layer.

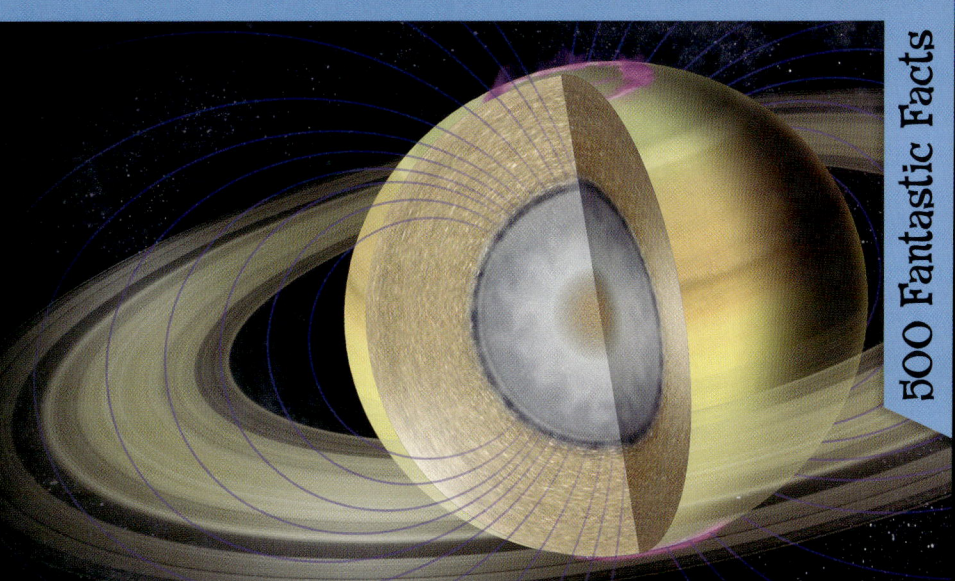

418 Saturn has a simple yet powerful magnetic field, which is formed by the currents in the liquid metallic hydrogen layer. Saturn's magnetic field is almost perfectly aligned with the planet's axis of rotation.

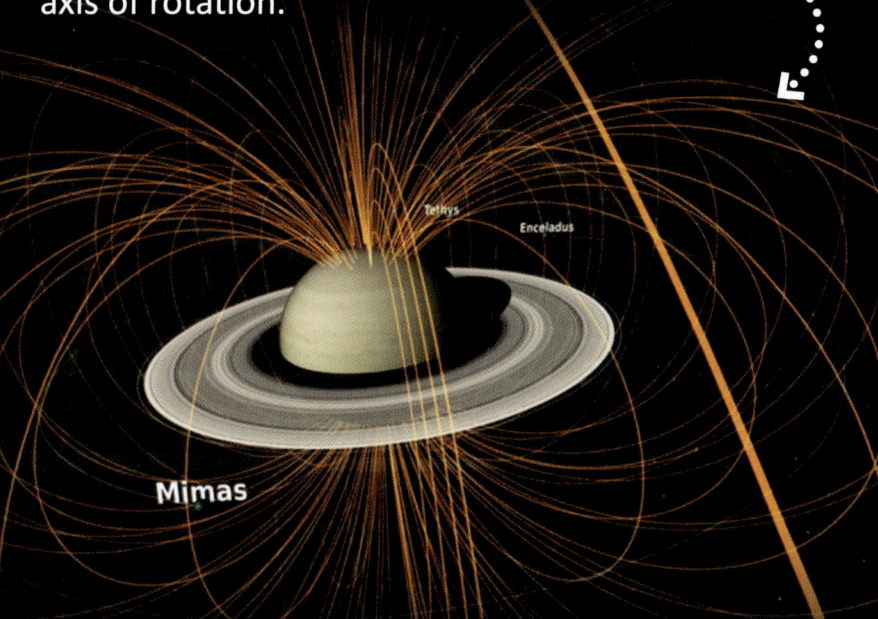

419 Saturn is a freezing cold place with temperatures measured in the range of -178°C to -185°C. However, its south pole has a warm polar vortex having temperatures as high as -122°C. It is thought to be the warmest point on Saturn. Instead of the Sun, the planet's interior generates most of its heat.

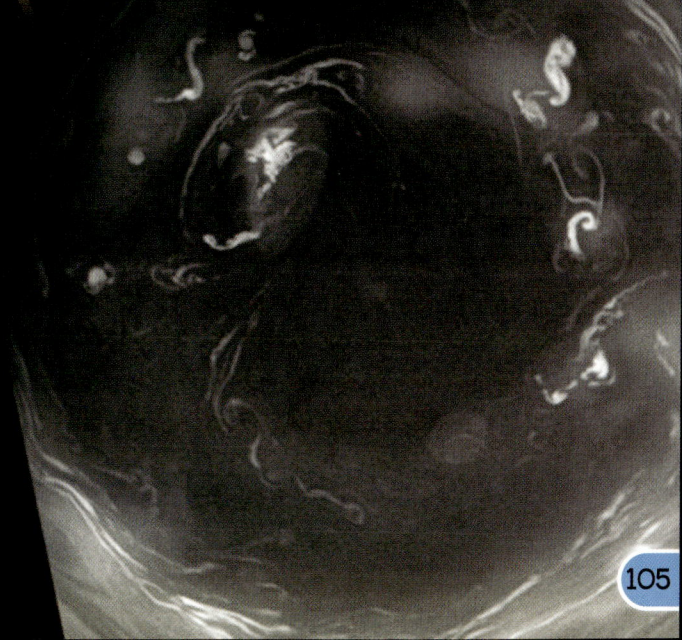

420 The clouds on Saturn look like jet streams. There are three cloud decks on Saturn: one is made of ammonia, one of ammonia hydrosulphide and one is water cloud. Storms and faint stripes give the planet different shades of grey, yellow, and brown. After Neptune, Saturn has the fastest winds in the solar system, with speeds reaching up to 1,110 miles per hour.

Saturn 2

421 A unique phenomenon called the "Great White Spot" is observed on Saturn once every 30 Earth years. It is a short-lived storm in Saturn's atmosphere that looks like a white oval on its surface. Earlier Great White Spots were seen in 1876, 1903, 1933, and 1960.

Visible Light (ISS)

Radio Signals (RSS)

422 The ring system of Saturn is its most notable characteristic. Despite not being the only planet with rings, Saturn possesses the most noticeable and extensive ring system.

423 Saturn's rings are assumed to be pieces of comets or asteroids, or pieces of a blasted moon broken apart by Saturn's gravity. They are composed of billions of tiny pieces of rock and ice along with dust. The particles in the debris range from dust-sized ice grains to pieces as big as a house.

424 Saturn's rings were first observed by Galileo in 1610, but as his telescope was not good enough, he thought them to be Saturn's moons. Later he assumed the rings to be some kind of "arms" of Saturn.

425 In 1655, it was Christiaan Huygens, a Dutch astronomer, who with the help of his improved telescope made an accurate deduction that the so-called arms were a kind of disc around Saturn. He described it as "a thin, flat ring, nowhere touching and inclined to the ecliptic".

426 The rings around Saturn are 270,000 kilometres wide. That is almost the same as the distance between Earth and Moon. However, these rings are very thin, measuring not more than 100 metres in thickness.

427 Saturn has four main groups of rings and three faint, narrow rings. These groups are separated by gaps called divisions. The Voyager spacecrafts, which flew by Saturn in 1980 and 1981, revealed that the seven ring groups are made up of thousands of smaller rings. The exact number is not known.

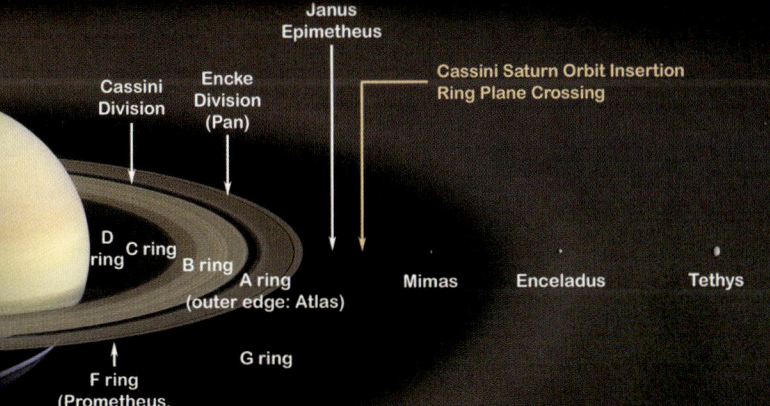

428 Saturn has an extremely strong magnetic field and displays auroras at its poles. The auroras are reddish in colour and ultraviolet in range because of the presence of hydrogen in the atmosphere.

Saturn's Moons

429 Among the planets in our solar system, Saturn has the most moons. Of the 82 known moons, 53 have been confirmed and given names while 29 are awaiting official naming and confirmation.

430 Saturn's first eight moons were discovered by using optical telescopes. Titan, the largest moon of Saturn and second largest in the solar system, was discovered on a refracting telescope by Christiaan Huygens in 1655.

431 Among all the moons in the solar system, only Titan has a worthwhile atmosphere. Titan features rivers, lakes, seas, and clouds that are filled with liquid hydrocarbons like methane and ethane. There is probably more water beneath Titan's thick water ice shell.

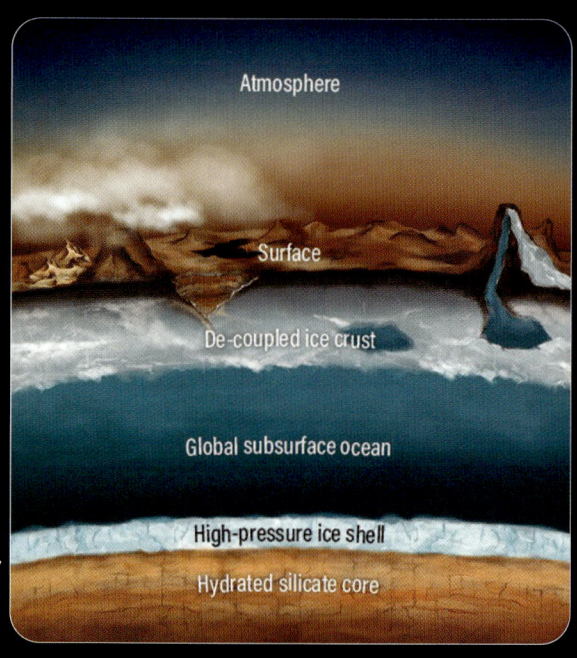

432 Titan has a thick and chemically active atmosphere having abundant organic compounds along with a considerable amount of hydrogen gas.

433 Enceladus, Saturn's icy moon, has a diameter of only 500 kilometres. It is one of the brightest moons in the solar system due to its ice-covered surface, which reflects the most sunlight. Enceladus contributes to Saturn's E ring material composition.

434 Over 96 percent of the mass in orbit around Saturn is made up from just one moon, Titan. Six moons smaller than Titan constitute approximately 4 percent of the mass and the remaining 0.04 percent is made up of 76 smaller moons together with the rings of Saturn.

Rhea   Iapetus

435 The other prominent moons of Saturn include Rhea, Iapetus, Tethys, Phoebe, Mimas, Dione, and Hyperion. The second and third biggest moons of Saturn are Rhea and Iapetus, respectively. They are both composed of three-quarters ice and one-quarter rock.

436 Epimetheus and Janus are referred to as co-orbital moons. Approximately similar in size, Janus is slightly bigger than Epimetheus. Only a few kilometres separate the orbits of Janus and Epimetheus. Every four years, their gravitational interaction causes them to swap orbits instead of colliding.

Epimetheus

Janus

Missions to Jupiter and Saturn

437 Pioneer 10 was the first spacecraft to fly by Jupiter and the asteroid belt in 1973. Voyager 1 and 2, in 1979, discovered Jupiter's faint rings, several new moons and volcanic activity on Io's surface.

438 The Galileo spacecraft was launched in October 1989, and it reached Jupiter's orbit in December 1995. It consisted of an orbiter and a probe. It was the first spacecraft to orbit an outer planet. It also captured the collision of fragments of comet Shoemaker-Levy 9 with Jupiter.

439 Juno became the second spacecraft to orbit Jupiter. It was launched in August 2011, and it reached Jupiter in July 2016. Its mission is to study the giant planet's atmosphere, structure, and magnetosphere. Jupiter will continue to be investigated by Juno until September 2025, or until the spacecraft's end of life.

440 Ulysses was jointly launched by NASA and ESA in 1990 with the intention of studying the Sun. However, in 1992, it passed Jupiter and studied its magnetosphere.

441 After Pioneer 11 in 1979, Voyager 1 and 2 flew past Saturn in 1980 and 1981 respectively. They investigated Titan and other moons, took pictures of the planet's rings, and studied the atmosphere's composition.

442 The Huygens probe of ESA landed on Saturn's moon, Titan, in 2005. It captured and relayed several images of Titan's surface and was able to estimate the atmosphere's composition and density.

443 NASA and ESA proposed the Titan Saturn System Mission (TSSM) to explore Saturn and its moons Titan and Enceladus. It was proposed to launch in 2020 and reach Saturn by 2029. A four-year prime mission would consist of two years of Saturn tours, two months of Titan aero-sampling, and a 20-month Titan orbit.

444 Cassini captured photos of Saturn's rings and moons. The mission also found the hydrocarbon lakes on Titan and the geysers on Enceladus. It also studied a storm that was occurring on Saturn.

Uranus

445 Uranus is the seventh planet from the Sun. It lies 2.6 billion kilometres from Earth when it is closest to it and 3.2 billion kilometres when it is farthest from it. Due to the great distance between the two planets Uranus is not visible to the naked eye. It was the first planet to be discovered through a telescope.

William Herschel

446 Uranus was discovered by astronomer William Herschel in 1781, but he initially thought it was a comet or a star. A later astronomer, Anders Johan Lexell, computed the orbit of the object and concluded that it was a planet and not a comet. The name "Uranus" for the planet was suggested by the astronomer Johann Elert Bode.

447 Uranus is also called the sideways planet because it rotates at nearly a 90° angle from the plane of its orbit. It makes the planet appear to orbit the Sun like a rolling ball. Uranus experiences 21 years of summer and 21 years of winter because of this peculiar tilt.

Titania

Oberon

Miranda

Puck

448 There are 27 known moons of Uranus. All of them are named from the works of William Shakespeare and Alexander Pope and are not based on any mythological characters.

Umbriel

Ariel

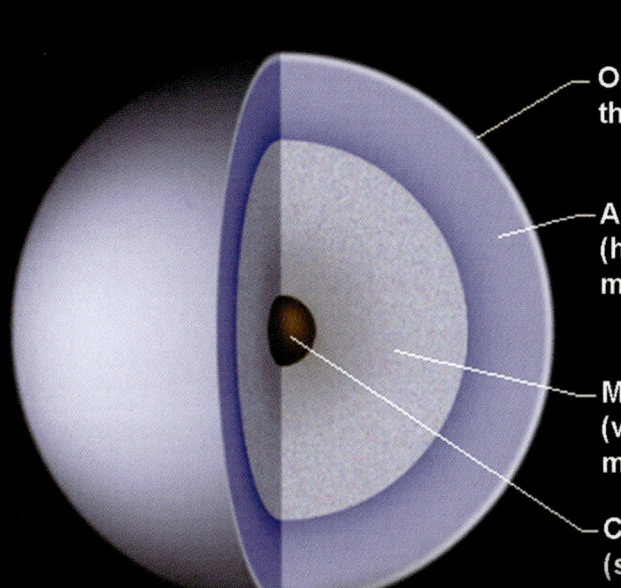

- Outer Atmosphere, the upper cloud layer
- Atmosphere (hydrogen, helium, methane gases)
- Mantle (water, ammonia, methane ices)
- Core (silicate/Fe-Ni rock)

449 A major part of the planet is made up of a hot, dense fluid of icy material consisting of water, ammonia, and other chemicals surrounding a small rocky core. The latest studies reveal that the central core is made up of iron and magnesium silicates.

450 Uranus has two faint sets of rings, outer and inner, discovered in 1977 by a group of astronomers. Presently, 13 distinct rings are known. It is believed a moon shattered by Uranus's gravity might have formed the rings.

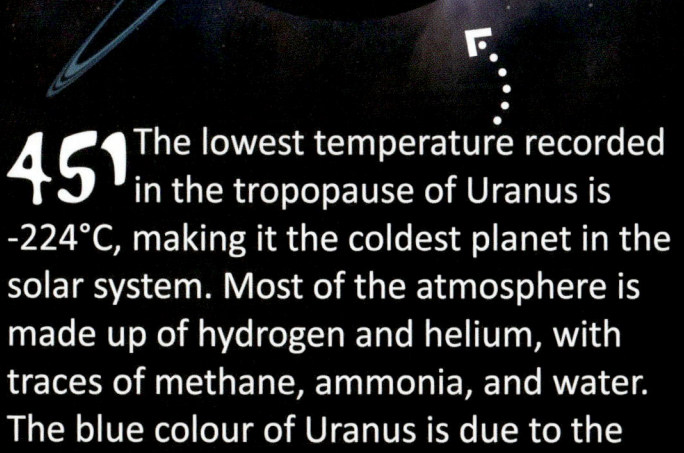

451 The lowest temperature recorded in the tropopause of Uranus is -224°C, making it the coldest planet in the solar system. Most of the atmosphere is made up of hydrogen and helium, with traces of methane, ammonia, and water. The blue colour of Uranus is due to the presence of methane.

452 A day on Uranus is 17 hours long. It takes the planet 84 Earth years to complete one revolution around the Sun. Uranus's magnetic field is 60 degrees away from its axis of rotation which makes the strength at its northern hemisphere ten times more than that at its southern hemisphere.

Neptune

453 The only planet whose discovery had been mathematically predicted before it was found was Neptune. In 1846, the French astronomer, Urbain Jean Joseph Le Verrier, calculated the location of Neptune. Around the same time, Johann Gottfried Galle, a German astronomer and Verrier's friend, observed the planet through his telescope and confirmed the prediction.

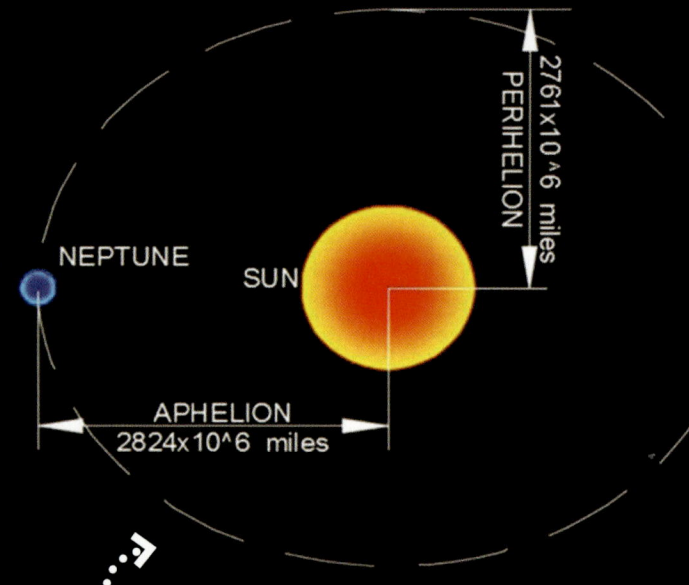

454 The distance between the Sun and Neptune is 4.5 billion kilometres which is 30 times the distance between Earth and the Sun. It takes the sunlight 4 hours to reach Neptune. One day on Neptune is 16 hours and it completes an orbit around the Sun in 165 Earth years.

455 In terms of physical size, Neptune is smallest among the gas giants but fourth largest in the solar system. It is an oblate spheroid, that is, its equator is wider than its poles. It has a diameter of 49,244 kilometres which is four times the diameter of Earth.

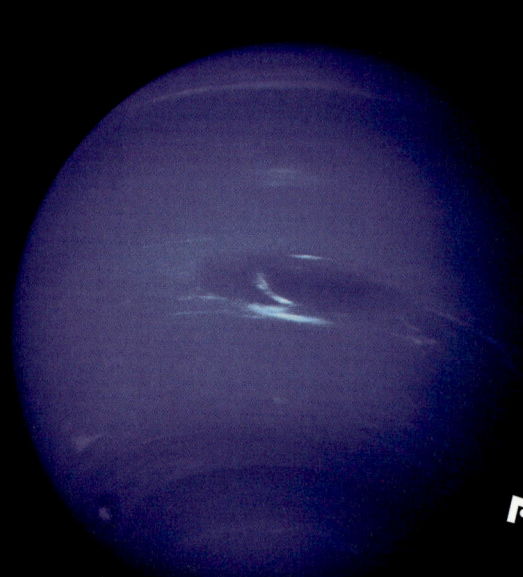

456 More than 80 percent of the planet's mass is made up of a hot dense fluid of "icy" materials comprising water, methane, and ammonia, surrounding a small, rocky core. There may be an ocean of very hot water under Neptune's cold clouds. Neptune's atmosphere consists mostly of hydrogen and helium and a small amount of methane.

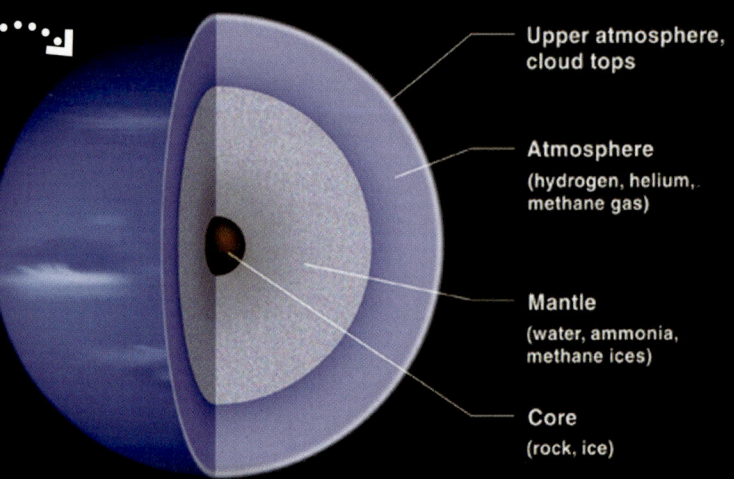

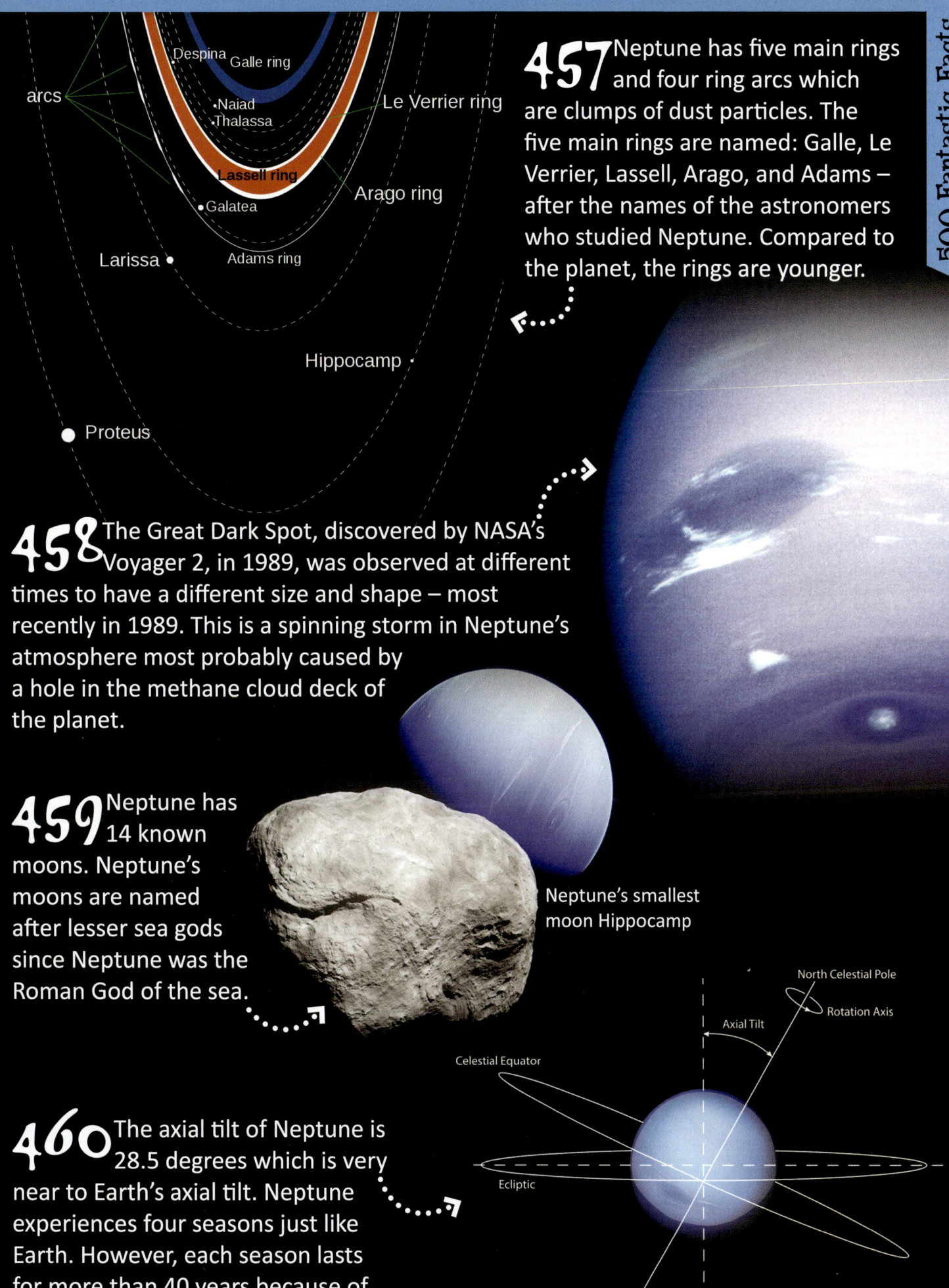

457 Neptune has five main rings and four ring arcs which are clumps of dust particles. The five main rings are named: Galle, Le Verrier, Lassell, Arago, and Adams – after the names of the astronomers who studied Neptune. Compared to the planet, the rings are younger.

458 The Great Dark Spot, discovered by NASA's Voyager 2, in 1989, was observed at different times to have a different size and shape – most recently in 1989. This is a spinning storm in Neptune's atmosphere most probably caused by a hole in the methane cloud deck of the planet.

459 Neptune has 14 known moons. Neptune's moons are named after lesser sea gods since Neptune was the Roman God of the sea.

Neptune's smallest moon Hippocamp

460 The axial tilt of Neptune is 28.5 degrees which is very near to Earth's axial tilt. Neptune experiences four seasons just like Earth. However, each season lasts for more than 40 years because of its large orbit around the Sun.

Moons of Uranus and Neptune

Miranda
Ariel
Umbriel
Oberon
Titania

461 Titania, Oberon, Umbriel, Ariel, and Miranda, are Uranus' five biggest moons. Titania, the largest moon orbiting Uranus, is also the eighth-largest moon in the solar system.

William Lassell

462 William Herschel discovered the two largest moons, Titania and Oberon, in 1787. Ariel and Umbriel were discovered in 1851 by English astronomer William Lassell. A century later, in 1948, Dutch astronomer Gerard Kuiper discovered Miranda, the smallest of the five large moons.

463 Uranus has 27 known moons. Some of them are as small as 12—16 kilometres and are nearly 4.8 billion kilometres away. Uranus's moons are divided into three groups: 13 inner moons, 5 major moons, and 9 irregular moons.

Gerard Kuiper

464 In 1986, the flyby of Voyager 2 resulted in the discovery of ten more moons of Uranus. Remaining moons were later found by the Hubble telescope and other modern ground-based telescopes.

Proteus

Hippocamp

Larissa

Galatea

Despina

Thalassa

Naiad

465 The moons of Neptune are divided into two categories: regular and irregular. Regular moons follow circular orbits around the planet. Irregular moons revolve around the planet in more eccentric, elliptical orbits. However, Triton orbits close to the planet in a nearly circular orbit.

466 Triton, Neptune's largest moon, has more than 99.5 percent of the total mass that orbits Neptune. It is the only known moon to orbit in a direction opposite to its planet's rotation. It is the coldest moon and very likely the coldest place in the solar system.

467 William Lassell discovered Triton, Neptune's largest moon, in 1846. Nereid was discovered by Gerard Kuiper in 1949 and, in 1981, Larissa was observed. In 1989, Voyager 2 found five inner moons and in 2001, five outer moons were discovered by two ground-based telescopes.

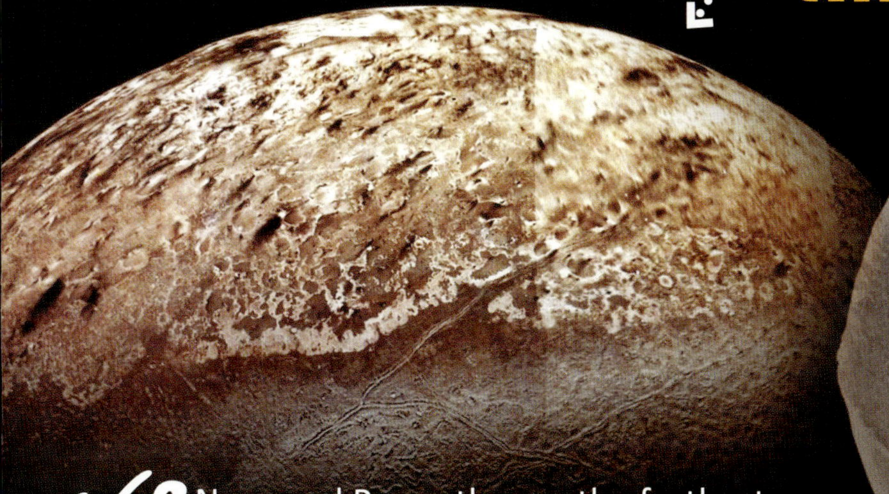

468 Neso and Psamathe are the furthest moons of Neptune. The most unusual thing about Neso is that it orbits its planet more distantly than any other known moon in the solar system.

500 Fantastic Facts

Missions to Uranus and Neptune

469 Voyager 2 is the first and only spacecraft to flyby Uranus and Neptune. It was designed to find and study the outer planets. Before exploring the ice giants, the spacecraft flew past gas giants Jupiter and Saturn.

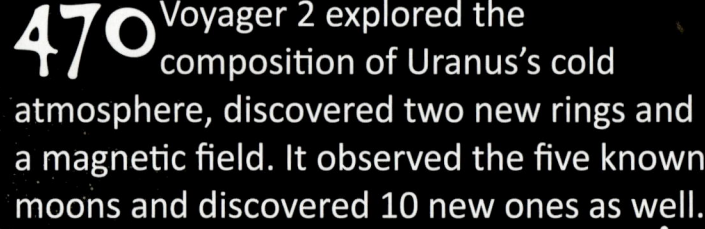

470 Voyager 2 explored the composition of Uranus's cold atmosphere, discovered two new rings and a magnetic field. It observed the five known moons and discovered 10 new ones as well.

471 On January 24, 1986, during a close flyby, Voyager 2 came within 81,500 kilometres of Uranus's cloud tops.

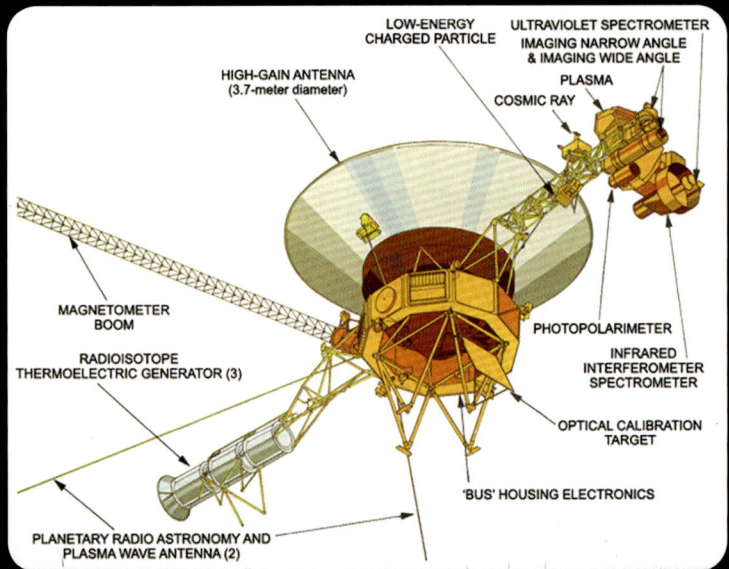

472 In addition to cameras, Voyager 2 is equipped with plenty of scientific equipment, including spectrometers, magnetometers, antennas, and power sources. However, as of 2021, many of these instruments have been shut off to conserve power while the spacecraft continues to travel through space.

473 On August 25, 1989, Voyager 2 passed about 4,950 kilometres above Neptune's north pole. It was the spacecraft's closest approach to any planet since it left Earth 12 years ago. It also made a close flyby of Triton, Neptune's largest moon, on the same day.

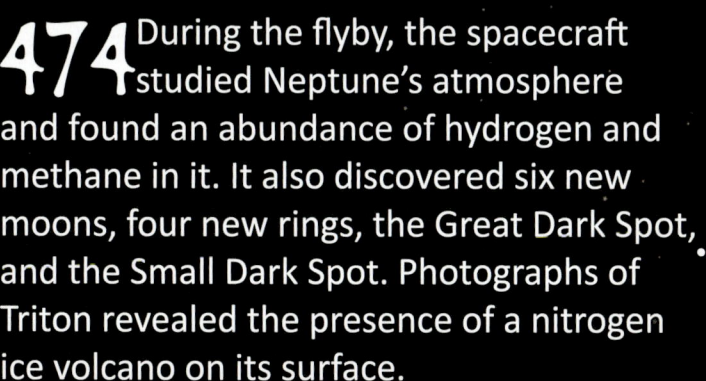

474 During the flyby, the spacecraft studied Neptune's atmosphere and found an abundance of hydrogen and methane in it. It also discovered six new moons, four new rings, the Great Dark Spot, and the Small Dark Spot. Photographs of Triton revealed the presence of a nitrogen ice volcano on its surface.

475 New Horizon was launched in January 2006 for Pluto. It crossed Uranus and Neptune on its way. It was in electronic sleep mode when it passed Uranus. It crossed Neptune in August 2014 and took pictures of Triton.

476 Some of the tentative future missions proposed for Uranus and Neptune include Uranus Orbiter and Probe, Uranus Pathfinder, OCEANUS, MUSE, Neptune Orbiter and Probe, Argo, New Horizons 2, and Trident.

Dwarf Planets

Pluto

477 As defined by the International Astronomical Union (IAU), a dwarf planet is a celestial entity that orbits the Sun, has enough mass to assume a roughly spherical shape, has not cleared other objects out of the area around its orbit, and is not a moon.

478 Pluto, which had been categorised as a planet since its discovery in 1930, was lowered to the status of a dwarf planet in August 2006 because it had not yet cleared the area around its orbit.

Earth

Pluto

Eris

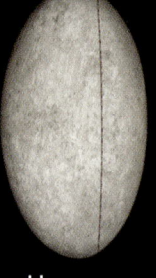
Haumea

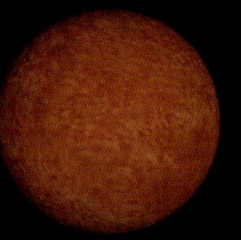
Makemake

Ceres

479 Pluto, Eris, Ceres, Haumea and Makemake are the five official dwarf planets, recognised by IAU. However, the scientific community also considers four more planetary objects as dwarf planets: Quaoar, Sedna, Orcus, and Gonggong.

480 Ceres is the smallest among the recognised dwarf planets. It was discovered in 1801 by Italian astronomer, Giuseppe Piazzi, and was believed to be an asteroid until 2006. Ceres is situated in the asteroid belt between Mars and Jupiter and is the closest dwarf planet to Earth.

481 American astronomer, Clyde Tombaugh, discovered Pluto in 1930. Eris was discovered by Mike Brown in 2005 (from data obtained in 2003), Haumea was discovered in 2004 and Makemake in 2005 by a team of American astronomers.

Mike Brown

483 Haumea has an unusual shape of an elongated ellipsoid because of its high speed of rotation. Recently, a ring has been found around this dwarf planet. As the ring is too faint to be studied, scientists use mathematical calculations to learn more about it.

482 Among the dwarf planets, Pluto has the most moons. Its five moons are Charon, Nix, Hydra, Styx, and Kerberos. Eris has a single small moon called Dysnomia. The two moons of Haumea are Namaka and Hi'aka, and Makemake has one provisional moon simply nicknamed MK 2.

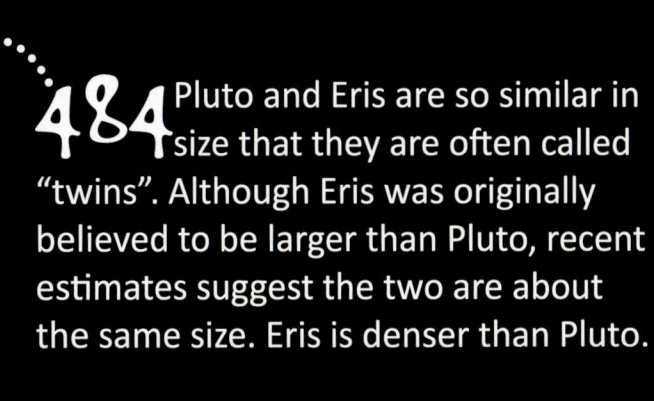

484 Pluto and Eris are so similar in size that they are often called "twins". Although Eris was originally believed to be larger than Pluto, recent estimates suggest the two are about the same size. Eris is denser than Pluto.

International Space Station

485 The International Space Station (ISS) is a large spacecraft that is orbiting Earth. It was built for continuous space exploration from low Earth orbit. It is a large science laboratory where astronomers and scientists reside. It also acts as a staging base for space missions.

486 The ISS is a collaborative project involving five space agencies: NASA (United States), ROSCOSMOS (Russia), JAXA (Japan), ESA (Europe), and CSA (Canada). The station is divided into two sections: the Russian Orbital Segment (ROS) and the United States Orbital Segment. The Russian segment includes six modules while the US segment includes ten modules.

487 The first residential crew arrived on ISS on November 2, 2000. Astronaut Bill Shepherd from the USA and cosmonauts Yuri Gidzenko and Sergei Krikalev from Russia were the first three people to live on the ISS.

488 The International Space Station (ISS) can be seen in the sky on a clear night, looking like a fast-moving star. Normally, it vanishes as swiftly as it appears.

489 On ISS, astronauts typically conduct laboratory studies, maintain, repair, and fix damaged equipment, clean their workstation, eat three times a day, and exercise for at least 2 to 2.5 hours each day. They work five days a week and get days off as well.

490 The assembly of the ISS began in 1998 with the launching of Russian modules robotically. The other pieces were delivered by space shuttles and installed by crewmembers. In 2000, the station was ready to have people on board. With the addition of several more modules, the station was finally completed in 2011.

491 ISS is 109 metres long and 75 metres wide (the area of a football field). It can accommodate six astronauts and a few visitors at a time. Two thirds of the station is used for research labs and storage. The laboratory modules are from USA, Russia, Europe, and Japan.

492 The space station is orbiting Earth at a speed of 17,500 mph. Astronauts onboard the station circle Earth every 90 minutes at that speed, witnessing 16 sunrises and sunsets in a 24-hour span. That means the crew is crossing 8 kilometres of space every single second.

Famous Astronauts

493 The Soviet cosmonaut, Yuri Gagarin, will always be remembered in history as the first man in space. Gagarin was a pilot in the Soviet Air Force. In 1961, Gagarin completed an orbit around Earth in the Vostok 1 capsule. For this achievement he was awarded the title of "Hero of the Soviet Union". Gagarin tragically died in 1968 during a routine training flight.

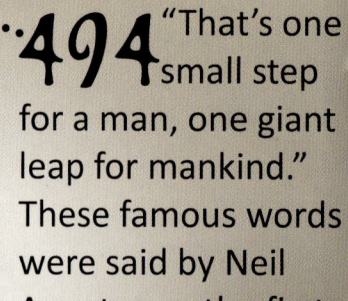

494 "That's one small step for a man, one giant leap for mankind." These famous words were said by Neil Armstrong, the first man to "set foot" on the Moon. He, along with Buzz Aldrin and Michael Collins, became the first manned mission to the Moon on July 16, 1969. The success of Apollo 11 mission gave the space programs new hope.

495 Sally Ride was the first American woman to fly in space on June 18, 1983. She was an astronaut on a space shuttle mission. Her responsibility was to employ a robotic arm to help put satellites into space. In 1984, she took off once more on the space shuttle and then quit NASA in 1987.

496 Just 23 days after Gagarin's first space flight, on May 5, 1961, Alan Shepard became the first American to travel into space in his mercury capsule named Freedom 7 during a suborbital flight. Shepard did not orbit Earth, his flight lasted for only 15 and a half minutes. He was also the fifth astronaut to walk on the Moon.

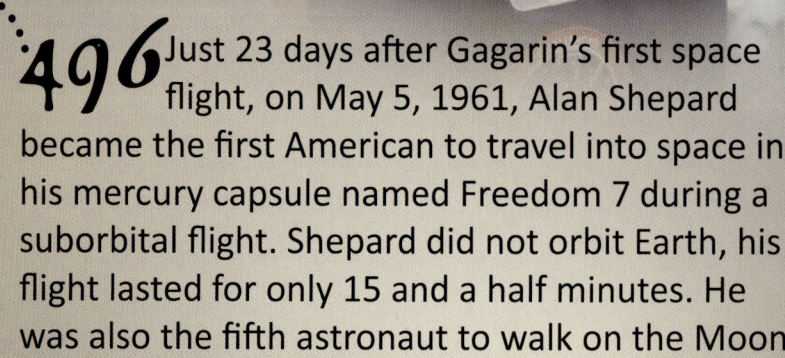

497 On June 16, 1963, Russian cosmonaut Valentina Tereshkova became the first woman in space. In her Vostok 6 capsule, she spent almost three days in space and orbited Earth 48 times. Despite having no piloting experience, she was accepted into the program because of her 126 parachute jumps.

498 Canadian astronaut, Chris Hadfield is one of the most famous astronauts who has a large fan following. He made a total of three trips to space: Russian *Mir* in 1995 and ISS in 2012 and 2013. Onboard the ISS, he even recorded a song and released it on Christmas Eve!

499 Kalpana Chawla was the first female of Indian origin to go to space. She joined the NASA Astronaut Corps in 1995, and a year after that she flew on her first space mission. While returning from her second trip in 2001, her shuttle disintegrated upon re-entering the atmosphere. All seven members of the mission lost their lives, including Kalpana.

500 Alexei Leonov, was one of the most loved cosmonauts in the former Soviet Union. On March 18, 1965, he became the first person to perform a spacewalk outside his capsule for 12 minutes and 9 seconds. His second trip into space was in 1975, as commander of Soyuz 19 of the Apollo-Soyuz mission.